A Special Amish Joy

Hannah Winstone

Published by Trellis Publishing, 2021.

A SPECIAL AMISH JOY

First edition. July 3, 2021.

Copyright © 2021 Hannah Winstone.

ISBN: 979-8224853618

Written by Hannah Winstone.

A SPECIAL AMISH JOY

HANNAH WINSTONE

Judith fidgeted as she stood beside her mother, small hands clasped in front as she stared ahead. *This isn't forever,* she reminded herself for the dozenth time that day, *just until Father gets out of the hospital and Mother gets her strength back.*

But Mother had been ill for months, and now Father was too. It had been nice at first, with just Judith and her mother in the house; but Mother couldn't look after her alone.

So there she stood, staring up at an unfamiliar house, on an unfamiliar porch, about to meet the people she would be living with for the foreseeable future.

"You'll do just fine," her mother, Dorothea, reassured, "I promise, as soon as I'm well again you'll be able to come straight home."

Judith simply shrugged, eyes darting to the ground. She didn't look up again until the door unlatched - and then her eyes snapped up, growing wide as they landed on a tall, slender woman.

The woman beamed, stepping forward to offer an outstretched hand to Dorothea. They embraced as if they were old friends - yet Judith didn't know this woman at all. "Good evening, Dorothea," she chirped, "how are you feeling? Better, I hope. And this must be little Judith! It's so nice to meet you, dear."

In reply, Judith offered a simple wave.

"Come inside, both of you. I'll make us all tea - or do you prefer coffee nowadays, Dorothea? It's been so long-"

"Actually..." Dorothea flushed, averting her gaze. She was so pale and thin, even just standing seemed to take physical effort. Judith noticed how she was leaning against the door frame, arm shaking. "I have to get back, and it's such a long way to go on foot... I was planning to stop by the hospital, but it would mean taking a bus and you know how I hate leaving the village.."

"I'll be fine," Judith muttered. A tiny hand came up to tug her mother's sleeve, dark eyes imploring. "You need to rest. That's why I'm here, isn't it?"

She didn't *want* her mother to leave - but eventually Dorothea was forced to. She kissed Judith's cheek, shaking as she straightened out again, and offered an uneasy wave. "You be good for the Miller's now. And don't you worry about me."

It was impossible not to, when each step was shakier than the last and Dorothea's face was so frightfully pale. She waved goodbye, heaviness settling into the pit of her stomach as she watched her mother disappear.

The woman's warm hand offered comfort as she led Judith inside. "You can call me Myra," she spoke softly, "and my husband is called Cyrus. We have a son too, the same age as you, and I hope you'll get on."

The words barely registered as Judith allowed herself to be towed into the kitchen. She was exhausted and hungry - but that all paled in comparison to the emptiness in her gut. Already she wanted her mother back.

"...speaking of, here they are now!"

Judith's head snapped up, loose curls blowing into her dark eyes, and she locked gazes with a short, stocky boy. He looked about eight - maybe a *little* older, if his broad shoulders were any sign - and he grinned at her with a mouth full of gap teeth. "You're Judith, rigth?" he questioned with a smile, "I'm Simon. Do you want me to show you your new room?"

"*Simon,*" a voice complained - and a tall, dark haired man appeared from the room beyond the kitchen, "this poor girl needs rest, not you running her ragged." He turned to Judith then, and his smile was the spitting image of Simon. "I'm Cyrus, lovely to meet you Judith. Did your mother not stop by?"

"She had to go," Judith mumbled, "she's too sick to be outside for long."

Cyrus' smile faded, sympathy overtaking his strong features. When he exhaled, he seemed defeated. "Well, we all get sick sometimes," he admonished, "she'll be better soon. Your father too, I'm sure."

Judith's father, Tobias, was a strong man - too strong, in her opinion. He would recover in a matter of weeks no doubt; something like pneumonia was nothing to him. If only he had caught something worse, something to keep him in hospital for months or even years...

A spark of guilt ignited in her chest, cheeks flushed as she snapped back to reality. "I'm sorry, but I'm very tired. Would it be all right if I went straight to sleep?"

"Of course," Myra replied gently, "Simon, help Judith with her bags, would you?"

Diligently, Simon scooped up her bags - only two, since she wasn't supposed to be here longer than a month. They seemed weightless in his arms as he grinned over at her, hoisting one bag over his shoulder. "Come on, your room is upstairs. It's usually our spare, but it's been made up specially!"

She followed silently, head ducked low as she sent a grateful smile toward Myra and Cyrus. Simon led her up a rickety, staircase, through a long hallway, until they reached a room right at the end. The place was maze-like - not big by any means, but long and narrow and twisting.

"Here we are!" Simon announced, dropping her bags unceremoniously at the door. Then he flushed, darting down to arrange them in *some* semblance of neatness.

At the same time Judith crouched, grabbing the strap of her satchel out of Simon's grasp. "Be more gentle," she muttered, stretching out to nudge them into the room.

"I'm sorry!" Simon apologised, and it might have been cute how crimson his face had turned, if not for his wide eyes fixed on her.

"What is it?"

"I..." he squinted, pointing toward her still outstretched arm. "Are you all right? That looks painful."

Painful? What was he... *oh*. Judith's gaze landed on her arm, where her sleeve had ridden up to reveal an array of yellowed bruises from wrist to elbow. They were old, too old to cause any pain, and certainly not the worst she had received. With a glare she pulled down her sleeve and darted to her feet. "I'm fine," she snapped, "but I'm tired, so I'd like to be alone now."

Simon frowned, eyes still lingering on her now covered arm. "If you're sure," he replied, "but I should tell my parents about-"

"You *won't,*" she shot back, "just... please. I'm tired, and worried about my parents, and I want to sleep."

Their eyes met, briefly, and she was struck by how bright and warm those green eyes of his were. Then Simon shrugged, sending her an apologetic smile, and left.

Judith tried not to think about him as she changed into a nightgown, tried not to think about the healing bruises on her arms. He was sweet, but getting involved with her family was never a good idea.

————————————————

The days passed uneventfully, after that. Judith discovered that she actually *liked* Simon, when he wasn't asking nosy questions. She was kept busy enough to avoid thinking about her parents, and that was fine by her.

She sat on the garden swing; an old, creaky wooden thing tied to the enormous oak tree outside the Miller's property. She swung gently, propelled more by the chilly breeze than from actually trying. It was a lot nicer than the back yard she had at home; hers was overgrown with weeds, the back porch used more for storing old junk than anything else.

Mother was too sick to garden; and before Father had been sent to the hospital, he had been too busy with such trivial things. His words, not hers. Judith would have *loved* a garden as neat and attractive as the Millers'.

"Daydreaming again?"

Dark eyes snapped up, landing on Simon's smiling face as he offered a glass of fresh lemonade. Judith took it silently, offering only a nod as thanks. The glass was cold, damp with condensation, but when she took a sip it was delightfully sweet. Far sweeter than anything she was used to - Father *abhorred* anything he considered an indulgence.

Simon flopped down onto the grass across from her, his own glass in hand. "Ma says dinner will be ready soon," he informed with a smile, "aren't you cold out here? You don't even have a coat."

Judith shrugged. She could have grabbed her shawl from the coat stand on her way out, but it hadn't been cold at the time. She had a scarf, though - a nice grey and green one Myra had given her.

But apparently, Simon wasn't satisfied. He wrestled off his own coat, standing to drape it across Judith's narrow shoulders. "There," he stated, "all better!"

She had to admit it *was* cosy; thick and warm, if too big around the middle. Judith buried her face into it anyway, soaking up the familiar scent of home cooking - no doubt from dinner inside - and that specific smell that was decidedly *Simon*. "Thanks," she muttered into the coat, "it *is* kind of chilly."

"It's nearly October, what do you expect!" Simon laughed - it was an oddly raspy sound, strange from a kid the same age as herself. Yet Judith found herself smiling too as he continued, "maybe I could ask Ma to get you a warmed coat? All you have is that shawl and a couple of cardigans."

A frown creased at her forehead then, lips tilting down. "My *mother* made me that shawl," she murmured, "and Father gifted me most of those cardigans." And with her father, gifts were rare. She had learned to treasure them as if they were gold; or pay the price.

Simon shifted, mouth opening as if to say more - but then Myra's grinning face peered from the door, a hand ushering them inside. "Dinner is almost ready. Come inside and wash your hands."

"Yes, Ma!" Simon called, twisting around to cast Myra a beaming smile. His enthusiastic nod sent blonde hair flying into his eyes. Laughing, he turned back to Judith - and then his smile dropped.

Did she *really* look so sour? Judith tucked a stray strand of hair behind her ear, gaze downcast.

"Is something wrong?"

No."

"You *look* like there's something wrong."

Tugging the oversized coat tighter around her narrow shoulders, Judith scowled. "Do you ever stop asking questions?"

"Not when there's questions that need to be asked."

Judith shoved down the irritation bubbling underneath her skin. She barely knew this boy, had no reason to let him affect her like this... yet despite the way he made her so incredibly *angry,* she was grateful for his company. She didn't want to be alone.

"Kids, *dinner,*" Cyrus yelled from inside.

Judith flinched, heart skipping as her eyes snapped toward the door. Disobeying *Myra* was one thing - but Cyrus? They had to go inside right now-

But Simon only huffed, heaving himself to his feet to offer a hand. "Don't look so *afraid.* My Dad's not going to be mad. Come on - don't forget your lemonade!"

Judith forced herself to relax. She was *fine,* and they were *fine.* Her Dad wasn't here to yell or throw things; and she had never even heard Cyrus get angry once. With a nervous smile, she allowed him to tug her from the swing and lead her inside.

Myra smiled as she set a steaming pot of vegetables onto the kitchen table. "About time," she huffed, "wash your hands, and come sit down."

Judith immediately darted to the sink, enjoying the warm water rush over her chilled hands. She washed them with soap, lingering in

the warmth just a *little* longer than necessary. When she turned to fetch a kitchen towel, her stomach flipped.

Simon was whispering to his mother. It was mostly quiet, indiscernible, but definitely about *her*. Judith recognised her name, heard whispers about her bruised arms and timid demeanour.

After a moment Myra's gaze darted over - and when she realised she had been caught, Myra smiled uneasily. "Done, dear?"

There was no mention of the whispers, or of the Miller's apparent concern for her well being; but uneasiness grew within Judith's chest all the same.

———————————————

Judith smiled, a basket of fresh produce bouncing on her hip as she wandered down the street. The market had been busy - too busy for two children to go themselves, perhaps - but the cool air against her skin was refreshing, and the sun had decided to peek through the clouds just for the occasion.

"Did we get everything?"

"I think so." Simon glanced down at the list Myra had written for him. "We have eggs, bread, vegetables... oh, we forgot the apples for the pie!"

Judith winced, her eyes darting down to inspect the basket. Sure enough, they had forgotten apples. "We could go back," she suggested quietly, "it won't take long."

"We're already home," Simon chided. They turned the corner together, the Miller property swimming into view as they approached. "Ma won't mind, and - wait, who's that on the porch?"

Judith's hand froze over the wooden gate, dark gaze widening as she caught sight of the tall, muscular man standing on the Milers' porch. Already? But she had only been here for two weeks, he wasn't supposed to be out of the hospital until the end of the month.

"Judith, are you all right?"

A soft hand landed on her shoulder, Simon's concerned gaze filling her vision. Judith flinched, a gasp leaving her lips - and then her father was turning around, his dark gaze locking onto hers.

"Ah, Judith! Where have you been? I'm here to take you home." He stretched out an arm, beckoning her forward - but instead of joining her father's side Judith danced around him. He scowled, reaching out to grab her arm as she tried to slink past. "Now Judith, that isn't the way to greet your father, is it?"

"Don't!" she snapped as his arm clamped around her bruised arm. The bruises themselves no longer hurt but his grip *burned,* like she had been set alight by his touch.

The door swung open then, Myra's freckled face falling into a frown as she saw the scene. "Judith, Simon, what's going on?"

"I'm here to take my daughter back," Tobias snapped, "I'm Tobias Lambright. Judith's father."

Myra's gaze wandered from his scowling features, down to the dirty shirt he wore, before landing on the broad hand clamped painfully around Judith's slender wrist. "It doesn't look like Judith wants to go home," she replied, "so why don't you let her go? Simon, Judith, come inside."

Simon scampered up the porch steps, reaching for Judith's free hand as he slipped past. She reached for him too, the basket dangling dangerously from her one free wrist.

Yet Tobias didn't let her go. In fact he only held on tighter, so tightly Judith's wrist began to *ache.* She twisted in his grasp, but it only served to cause a shooting pain along her arm. Her heart thudded in her chest, stomach squirming. If she went home with him now, while her mother was still weak and she was alone with him... bruises would be the least of her troubles.

"Mister Lambright," Myra snapped - and she was such a sweet, kindly woman but in that moment her expression was *dark.* "You had better let her go right this moment, or I'll call my husband over. Better yet, I'll contact the police."

Judith didn't have to look to see his expression. She knew it well - *too* well. Narrowed eyes, pursed lips, crinkled nose. The kind of scowl only a truly horrible man could muster. "She belongs to *me,* and that's the end of it," he growled - and pulled Judith to him with enough force she cried out, wincing as his thick arms wrapped about her shoulders in a mockery of fatherly protection.

Simon's eyes were wide as Judith looked at him. Something had clicked in his mind, and with a jolt of panic Judith realised he finally understood what was going on. Tiny fists clenched, his bright eyes narrowing, and he stepped past his mother to look at Judith. His expression softened a little, voice sympathetic as he asked, "Judith, do you want to go home? Or do you want to stay with us?"

Her eyes darted up to her father, tears threatening to spill over her cheeks. She blinked them away, nose curling. "I want to stay," she mumbled, turning back to Simon. His presence was calming, somehow, even with Tobias' vice like grip digging into her skin and his glare boring into her.

"Then it's settled," Myra replied with a nod, "she will stay right here for as long as she wants. Now *let her go.*"

She expected a protest - shouting, swearing, the threat of fists. Yet Tobias' grip lessened as he practically threw Judith toward Myra with a grunt of disgust. "Fine, keep the brat, if you like her that much. But Judith belongs to *me,* and I will have her back. I'll be back tomorrow, and you had better be ready."

His gaze lingered on Judith and she shivered. She watched Tobias spin on his heel and storm down the porch steps. His feet crunched along the gravel path and he threw open the gate, letting it clatter shut with an ear-ringing bang.

Judith hadn't realised she was shaking, not until Simon's warm hand reached for hers. He led her inside without a word - but Judith didn't miss the knowing look he shared with his mother. He sat her down at the kitchen table, muttering reassurances she didn't quite hear.

Myra slid a steaming cup of tea across the table - but even the warmth from the hot drink couldn't stop her shivers. Judith clutched the cup as if it were her lifeline, head bowed until loose curls fell into her eyes.

"Judith, dear?"

She winced, folding in on herself like it would make her disappear. She *wanted to,* so desperately it was overwhelming. She had avoided him for today - but Father would be back. Then what? Things would just go back to how they were? With an awful father and a mother who couldn't do anything to stop it? What if-

"Dear, we saw what happened out there. You need to tell us everything. Has... has your father been hurting you?"

She shifted under the intensity of their gaze. She wanted to cry, but her tears had dried up, leaving behind only a sense of emptiness. Resignation.

"Judith," Simon murmured, reaching out to cup her hand in his, "please? We want to help. *I* want to help."

Oh, how could she say no to that? Her eyes flickered up, landing on his softly smiling face, pale skin flushed from the cold. Myra, too, was looking at her with such fondness it was almost painful. So Judith didn't have a choice but to tell them, really.

"He never used to be," Judith mumbled, "but then Mother got sick, and he had to work harder and harder to make up for it. He just... he gets so stressed, having to look after us both *and* work extra hours." She ducked, cheeks flushing crimson. Here she was, making *excuses* for him when he was the reason her arms were covered in faded bruises. "Father he... he takes his anger out on me. It's better than him hurting Mother; she's been sick for so long - not like Father, he got better. But Mother... her illness isn't something that goes away."

Myra's sigh was sympathetic, her blue eyes creasing into faint crow's feet. "Oh, sweetheart, I'm so sorry."

"We won't let him take you!" Simon argued, "if he tries, we'll stop him."

"I'll speak to Dorothea. She *must* know what Tobias has been doing."

Judith cringed. The steam from the tea was beginning to cool, the mug no longer hot to touch. Yet she clung to it, hands turning white from the remaining heat. "She can't stop him," Judith mumbled. Once again tears bubbled at the edge of her vision - it seemed she only cried when she didn't *want to.* Swiping under her eyes, she tried not to let them fall. "We're stuck with him, because he's the only one that can look after us both."

Simon squeezed her hand, his expression soft. "You and your mother could both live with us. Couldn't they, Ma?" His gaze darted up, wide and hopeful.

Myra pursed her lips, eyes glancing from Simon to Judith, then back again. "I don't know, dear, but I *do* know that we won't let him hurt you again. No child should be put through that." She reached out to brush a strand of hair from Judith's face, smile playing on her gentle face. "Your mother and I have been good friends for years, and she never said a thing about *any* of this. I had my suspicions, but..."

"But she's very good at pretending everything is okay," Judith finished quietly. It was true; Dorothea was the kind of woman who pretended nothing was wrong right until the last moment. It was part of the reason why she was so sick; ignoring symptoms, using home remedies even when it became clear they didn't work. She ignored modern medicine because of her - *their* - principles. But look where it got them all.

Silence fell over the three, then. Judith let her gaze fall back to the table, pretending as if the grooves and stains in the wood were the most fascinating things she had ever seen. For a while it was as if no one was going to speak - no one knew *what* to say, least of all Judith herself.

Simon, a solid form of reassurance beside her, shifted awkwardly. He let out a little sigh, hand squeezing hers for the millionth time. Then, he said, "that first day, when I asked about your bruises. I knew something was wrong. I should have done something, instead of just ignoring it-"

"Don't blame yourself," she replied with a huff, "you didn't know. I didn't *want* you to." She smiled weakly, eyes not quite meeting his. "I didn't know you then, didn't know if you were worried or just being nosy."

"I'm *not* nosy," Simon accused - only for Myra to laugh. "I'm not!"

"Simon Josiah Miller, you're the nosiest person I've ever known," Myra retorted with a roll of bright blue eyes. "Ask anyone, they'll say the same."

Something changed, then. The mood lifted, the tension in the room fled until all three of them were grinning broadly. Holding back a laugh, Judith said, "you ask too many questions, and you're too curious for your own good. Yes, you are."

Simon huffed, rolled his eyes, and sent Judith a dazzling smile. "It's why you like me."

Well, she couldn't very well *deny* that. Her cheeks flushed as she snatched her hand back - and stuck out her tongue. She *did* like him though, and not just for his natural curiosity. His bright smile, his generosity - and the way he always managed to cheer her up without even meaning to. Like now, for instance.

Yet her mind drifted back to her father, back to the bruises lacing her arms, and what that meant for her. Tomorrow, she'd be back with him.

No, she reminded herself, *Simon and his family won't let him take me. They have a plan.* Or at least, she hoped so.

Myra's smile was kind as she stood, ruffling both Judith and Simon's hair as she passed them. "I suppose I should start lunch," she mentioned idly, "thank you for going to the market today. We can talk more about this later; but things always seem better with a full stomach. Don't you agree?"

Judith simply smiled, her nod bouncing those thick curls. And so the day continued as normal, and Judith felt like she belonged.

————————————

Judith had spent almost the entire day curled up in what had become her favourite armchair, gazing out the window. She flinched every time a neighbour walked by, or a bird landed on the windowsill outside.

When her father finally *did* make his arrival, striding along the gravel path and up the porch steps, Judith watched with wide, cautious eyes. He announced himself by banging on the door, huge knuckles on wood, and shouting Judith's name.

Myra was the one to answer. Simon and Cyrus hovered by Judith's side, ready to step into action if the situation called. Simon's hand fit firmly in hers as she heaved herself out of the armchair and inched into the hall.

"Judith, you're coming home with me immediately."

She sucked in a breath, eyes darting to Myra, then to Cyrus, before landing on Simon. Well, here came the moment of truth. "I don't want to."

"Girl, you listen-"

"Mr. Lambright," Myra interrupted. Her voice was so even, so unaffected, and her smile seemed so *genuine*. "Judith has decided she wants to stay with us. In fact, I would like to speak with Dorothea to-"

Tobias' expression darkened. "Dorothea is none of your business," he snarled, "you don't get to say her name."

Any normal person would have cowered under the intensity of his glare - but Myra remained calm. Other than the quirk of a dark brow, she didn't even react. "With all due respect, sir, I'd have to disagree. Dorothea-"

Suddenly Tobias lunged forward, little more than a blur, snatching Judith by the wrist. She let out a gasp as pain ricochet through her arm, still tender from the day before. "Dad!" she exclaimed - but it fell on deaf ears.

"You're coming home *right now,* and I won't hear another word of it. I have bad news."

Bad news? Judith stilled, even as her wrist ached, wide eyes staring up at Tobias. What did he mean by *bad news?* Everything was bad to him, and he always had a way of making something innocuous sound like the end of the world. But this... it was different.

Simon darted forward, linking his arm through Judith's. "Is this an excuse to get her to come home? It won't work."

Judith's heart was hammering in her chest, pulse racing. Tobias stared her down as if challenging her - his silence made her shiver. "What's the bad news?" she finally questioned, voice little more than a squeak.

He huffed, rolled his eyes, but there was something else in his gaze; something unfamiliar. *Worry.*

"Dad?"

Pursing his lips, Tobias gestured to the door. "You're mother is ill, and she needs you home *right now* to look after her."

Her insides squirmed. "Mother's been ill for years," she murmured, "that's why she has medicine from the big hospital." She didn't like it, of course, relying on outsiders to keep her at least somewhat healthy. But this wasn't news. So why...

"She's getting worse," Tobias snapped, "no doubt your fault, refusing to come home and giving her stress." He tugged on her arm once more, all but dragging her outside - and this time, Judith didn't fight it.

"Hey!" Simon darted forward, eyes wide as he stumbled over the uneven carpet. "You can't just drag her home-"

"It's all right," Judith murmured, "if... if Mother is ill, I need to see her." Had her illness finally caught up with her? Had Father somehow passed on *his* illness and made her worse?

Was she dying?

"I'll come with you," Myra and Simon ushered in unison, both rushing to Judith's side. In that instant she felt such a rush of warmth, if *love,* that it left her stunned. In only two weeks, these people had become her family.

Tobias didn't argue, simply storming on ahead, work boots grinding into the neat grass of the Millers' garden. Judith hurried after him, Simon and Myra close behind.

The four of them walked in silence, awkward and tense and *horrible,* but it seemed no one wanted to be the one to break it.

By the time they reached the Lambright house - a small, shabby house at the end of a street full of equally small, shabby houses - Judith was so anxious she thought she might pass out. She sprinted past Tobias and into the house, barely pausing to wrestle off her shawl before running to the stairs.

"Judith, wait!" Simon called after her - and suddenly he was by her side. A solid, warm comfort that brought a nervous smile to hr lips. "Let's all go up together, okay?"

"No. Myra and the kid stay downstairs," Tobias snapped, "Dorothea doesn't need people nosing around-"

"I'm her *friend,*" Myra interjected, "and Simon is my son."

A grunt. A look that asked *do you think I care?*

Eventually Myra relented, sending Judith an apologetic smile as she pulled Simon to her side. "Fine, but if you hurt her, I'll know."

Tobias jerked his head toward the steps. "Go on then." And then, since Judith clearly wasn't fast enough, he shoved her upstairs with a cold hand at her back.

Her parents' room sat at the end of a narrow hall, door slightly ajar. Judith rushed to it, shoving the door open and stumbling over the threshold. She caught her footing just in time, heart in her throat, gaze darting to the bed.

Her mother lay propped up on a bundle of pillows, blonde hair fanning across her pale face. Paler than Judith remembered. Thinner.

"Mother?"

Dorothea opened her arms wide, a wonderful smile stretching across her narrow face. "Judith! Come here, I've missed you. Did you enjoy your stay with the Millers?"

"I didn't want to leave," she mumbled, climbing onto the bed to join her mother. It dipped under her weight, and Judith curled into Dorothea's side. "Cyrus is so nice, and Myra is *so kind.*"

"What about Simon?"

"He's... *weird,*" Judith replied with a smirk, "but he's really fun. I like him."

"That woman, Myra, is downstairs," Tobias snapped. He hovered by the door, a towering and imposing figure, but didn't enter. "Didn't want to let Judith come, until she heard you were ill."

Dorothea's smile slipped, eyes narrowing. "I don't blame her. Nor do I blame Judith for wanting to stay."

He grunted, arms folded across his broad chest. "Not my fault the little brat doesn't want to listen."

"Tobias!"

Even frail and tiny, Dorothea was a force of nature. Perhaps that's why even a man like Father had a conscience. Without Mother, he surely would have been twice as bad.

Tobias simply rolled his eyes. "So, are you going to tell her? Or do I have to?"

"Tell me what?" Judith glanced up, locking gaze with her mother's dark, warm eyes. There were lines there Judith didn't remember, wrinkles that had appeared in their brief two weeks apart. For the first time, Dorothea looked her age.

"I'm afraid," Dorothea murmured, running a hand through Dorothea's hair, "that I have to stay at the hospital."

Judith frowned, head tilted to the side as confusion lit up her mind. "Like Father did? Will they make you better?"

A sigh escaped her lips, and simply shaking her head seemed to take so much effort. "Not exactly. What I have can't be cured in two weeks, love. I could be there for a very long time."

"But... it will make you better?"

A smile, worn but genuine. "Yes. I had a chat with the doctors, and Myra too. It seems they convinced me to do what I should have done a long time ago."

"But then... I'll be living alone with Father?"

She felt him bristle, even without watching. She glanced at him from the corner of her eyes, sinking deeper into Dorothea's embrace. Yet he didn't say a thing, simply watching them silently.

"You'll be staying with the Millers," Dorothea decided, "at least, until I'm back home."

Judith's heart leapt, eyes snapping wide. She couldn't believe it, *any* of it. Was she simply dreaming? It was the only explanation - but could her mind even make up something this ridiculous?

"But I don't *want* to stay with them forever!"

"It won't be forever," Dorothea assured, "just a few months. I spoke to Myra last night, and she agreed... if I need care when I'm out of the hospital, we can *both* live with them."

"Absolutely *not!*" Tobias bristled. He was enormous, filling up the entire doorway as his fist connected with the wall. Judith flinched back, ducking under the bed covers, but he kept going. "You think I'll allow this? You think I'll let you live with *strangers,* instead of with me, where you belong?"

Judith was shaking, but Dorothea remained even. "I let this go on for too long. I needed something to wake me up - and this was it. I won't allow you to hurt Judith any longer."

"I can keep you here," he snarled, "a kid and a woman even frailer than her child. You can't stop me."

"But the police could."

Judith blinked, eyes darting between her parents. Tobias was *fuming,* but Dorothea didn't seem to mind.

"I've been compiling evidence. Accounts of everything you've done over the years. I can give them to Myra for safekeeping - and if you try *anything,* she'll go straight to the police."

"You hate outsiders," Tobias snarled, "you wouldn't-"

"I don't hate them more than I love my daughter," Dorothea snapped - and Judith felt a rush of love for her mother. Love and *admiration* so strong the was floored.

Tobias backed away, feet tripping over the carpet. His eyes were wide, fearful, and Judith had never seen him like this. With a rush of guilt she realised - she *liked it.*

"Judith, go downstairs and tell the Millers' what I told you. Your father and I have to talk."

She hated to leave Mother alone with him, hated to leave her side at all after all she had been told - but she took a deep breath, nodded, and slipped from her side.

"Don't worry love, he won't do a thing, not now he knows I have evidence."

Judith slinked past Tobias, her heart hammering - but he didn't try to stop her. With one last glance toward her mother, Judith sprinted downstairs. She tripped over her skirts on the way, barely pausing to steady herself - and practically flew right into Simon's arms.

"Judith! Is everything okay?" He steadied her, thick hands braced against her narrow shoulders. His big eyes were concerned, lip parted in a silent question.

"Mother needs to go to hospital," she murmured, "your Ma knows everything. But... she says I can stay with you until she's better."

Simon smiled, uneasy but *genuine.* "I'm sorry she's ill," he replied, "but I'll be glad to see you stay!"

A laugh bubbled up in her chest, features splitting into a wide grin. "Me too! I was so worried, but I think everything is going to be okay now."

Her mother would be fine, once the doctors took care of her. Judith could stay with her new family, far away from the man that had hurt her for so long.

Yes, she was just fine despite it all.

Simon grinned and pulled her in for a hug so tight that for a moment, she forgot how to breathe. Then she was laughing, face buried in his shoulder as he lifted her from her feet.

Myra joined them, ruffling Judith's hair as Simon set her down. "You'll be all right with us," she murmured, "and when the time comes, your mother can join us too."

"Is your dad really all right with this?" Simon questioned.

A shrug, a smile. "He doesn't have a choice. Mother has been documenting everything, and I suppose she's using it to blackmail him." She turned to Myra, "she's going to give everything to you. Safekeeping, or something."

Myra paled - and then a grin overtook her face. Her laughter was musical, unrestrained in its delight. "Typical Dorothea!"

The three of them embraced right there in the hallway, Myra's long arms embracing both children as she shoved down her laughter.

Judith was safe from her father, for the first time in her life. She had a new, wonderful family - and soon her mother would be well again. Happiness swelled in her chest as she buried further into Simon's hug, and she smiled.

Chapter One

Abigail Stratsburger and her older sister were washing clothes in a dasher washer outside their house in the small town of Birchland, Pennsylvania. They usually did the washing on Fridays. It was such a familiar routine by now that Abbie could do it with her mind a million miles away. She and Beth were discussing Beth's upcoming wedding.

"Will you be having friendship cake?" Abbie asked.

"Oh we'll have everything," her sister Beth said. "I will miss teaching, I suppose."

"The children will miss you."

"Are you sure you don't want to replace me? They're looking for a teacher to fill my place. Not too far from home and free by three o'clock."

"But when would I work on my tapestries? I can't let the business go, you know. I've got to keep it running."

"Abbie, I just don't understand." Beth turned the handle in a steady rhythm. "The tapestries were *grandmam's* work and she loved it. But she's gone now. We'll miss her, jah, but you don't *have* to keep up her work. You won't be able to keep it going when you get married anyway."

Abbie reached into the washer and pulled some shirts from where they were tangled on the bottom. She shook her wet hands over the grass. "I may not get married for years and years. And I like having something of my own that belongs to *me*. I'd like to make a catalog of my tapestries. This way, the English *and* the Amish can order them by mail."

"If you keep talking in that bossy way of yours and declaring what you like and don't like, you may not ever get married. You're already twenty, you know. The fellows want a quiet and submissive spirit."

"I'll be quiet when I'm sitting in Sunday meeting. That's enough being quiet to last me all week," Abbie said. She started hanging the wet clothes on the clothesline strung up between two birches.

"When winter comes, we'll have to hang these up inside, you know. You'll have to move your *work* from the spare room."

"Winter's not here yet. There now, we're almost done and I'm going over to dawdi's house. I promised to stop by Friday."

Abbie made her way to her grandfather's house by foot, kicking the red and orange leaves out of the way. Her grandfather was a great friend of hers. He had grown mostly blind in the past year but his mind was clear as ever and Abbie went to him lots of times for advice. She also knew that he got lonely at times, missing *mommi,* and she wanted to keep him company.

As Abbie approached her grandfather's land, Blackie the shnauzer dog came running to greet her, yelping. Abbie opened the gate, patted Blackie, then straightened and stared.

There stood a large white van, so large it nearly blocked her view of her grandfather's house.

Aside from the occasional police car, Abbie had never vehicles in her community. She fixed her *kapp* and marched over to the van. She tried to understand where the car doors were, then realized that there was a door in the back, with two handles, instead of the ordinary trunk door. She reached over and knocked.

The door opened. A man in blue jeans and a dark blue t-shirt, with almond-shaped eyes studied her. He appeared Chinese at first glance, although Abbie couldn't be sure. He was standing up within the van with his head nearly touching the ceiling. She could hear music playing softly inside.

"Good morning."

Abbie exhaled. "I...I don't understand how you came to be here," she blurted out.

"I spoke to Elias Stratsburger. This is his land. He told me I could park my camper van on his property while I'm looking around for a more permanent place to stay."

"He didn't know your vehicle was so huge!" Abbie gasped. "You're taking up half the lawn. My grandfather is blind and you took advantage of that."

The man frowned. "I wasn't taking advantage. I'm paying him for use of his land. What does he care if it's a camper van or an ordinary car? Also, nice to meet you."

Abbie hesitated. Only then, it occurred to her that she'd shown a bit too much anger in speaking with a complete stranger. "Nice to meet you too."

"You've got a beautiful town. My name's Michael. I'll be staying awhile."

"Are you a writer?"

Michael blinked. "No. Do I look like a writer? I always thought writers had wire-rimmed glasses and slouched from sitting hunched over their computers."

"It's just...if you're not writing about the Amish," Abbie said. "I don't see why you're here."

Michael sighed. "I'm not entirely sure why I'm here myself. But I needed a place to park, so I found one. Want to come in for lunch?" He stepped aside to reveal eggs frying on a small gas stove right next to a cooler.

"Um...no, thank you. I'm actually on my way to my grandfather's to *make* lunch." And Abbie backed away. "Excuse me."

She had dealt with the English before. They could make great clients, yes. They could smile very brightly and ask how she was doing. But she'd had enough experience to learn that you couldn't trust them completely.

Her grandfather seemed entirely unruffled at the thought of someone living on his property.

"But dawdi, he might be dangerous," Abbie pleaded. "You can't see what he's doing out there all day."

'What could he be doing?"

"He might have a gun. He could end up shooting the rabbits that come grazing."

'Why shouldn't he? I can't shoot them anymore anyway."

'He might steal something."

"Abbie-girl, you look around and tell me if anything's missing. And tell your sisters to do the same when they come visiting. Now, sit down and tell me how your tapestries are coming along."

In the sunlit kitchen, with her grandfather placidly drinking tea, Abbie began to relax. "I've got two new designs I'm doing. One says 'An apple a day keeps the doctor away,' and another one says 'Family is forever.' The problem is that there just aren't that many customers."

"Why don't you sell them to one of those tourist shops in town? You'll make a little extra money and other people will be able to enjoy them."

"You know what I really want? I wish I could have a catalog, a nice, bright catalog with pictures, that I could mail out. And then people can mail-order what they want from all over Pennsylvania and I can ship it to them."

"Well, why don't you have one made and try it?"

"It might be expensive, getting something like that."

Abbie-girl, if you can explain to me in detail where every penny is going, down to the cost of stamps and bubble wrap, I'll help you fund it."

Abbie felt herself get all warm inside. "Really, dawdi? Honestly?"

"Why not? Now, why don't you go on out there and invite the stranger for some coffee."

"I don't think he needs my invitation. He's got a real kitchen inside of his van."

"Fine then." Her grandfather smiled. "Be stingy."

"*Stingy?* But -" Abbie sighed. "All right."

She walked over the browning grass to the camper van and knocked again.

The door opened. Michael was holding a newspaper in one hand and a steaming mug of coffee in another. "Hello again."

"We were going to invite you for some coffee," Abbie began. "But seeing how you've already got some, I doubt you'll want to come." She nearly turned around to leave.

"I'd love to come." Michael glanced back into the room for a minute, then tossed his newspaper onto a small couch and followed her, cup of coffee still in hand. "And you are Missis..."

"Miss Stratsburger. Most people call me Abigail."

"Are you the granddaughter that's getting married?"

"No, that's my sister," Abbie said. "Her wedding is on Tuesday."

"*Really?* How do you people communicate without phones around here?"

That seemed an odd switch in subject.

"We talk to each other," Abbie said.

"I mean...if I wanted to ask your sister's permission to come to her wedding, how would I ask her? Could I send her a written note?"

"The guest list is full already. I'm afraid there isn't space."

Michael sat drinking coffee and trying not to stare at Abigail too frankly.

He'd liked Elias instantly. A good, sociable, elderly man who had made a normal human agreement with Michael and had trusted him even though he wasn't Amish. But Abigail? Pretty as she was with her shiny dark braid falling just past her shoulder, and her blue eyes, she clearly didn't like him. Did she think he was there to make a documentary on the Amish without their permission? Did she just not trust men who weren't part of her church district? Or was she particularly suspicious with people who came from a different race? He couldn't tell.

He checked his cell phone quickly. No messages.

He glanced up. "Mr. Stratsburger, would you know if I can earn a little money while I'm staying here? I'm pretty good with my hands."

Elias smiled. "I'll have to ask. I used to own a business but passed it down to my nephew. He makes the decisions now. Abbie will ask for you, won't you, Abbie?"

"I'll ask. I've got to stop by in a few days anyway. He still has yet to pay me for my tapestry."

"You make tapestries?" Michael asked.

"Jah, to hang on the wall," Abbie explained, stirring sugar in her tea. "I've got thirty different designs, some of them with quotations, such as bible verses."

"And you make them all by hand?"

"I've got to if I want them to look right."

"I'd love to see them someday." Michael rose. "Well, I'm heading home. It was nice meeting you, Abbie."

For a moment, Abbie thought that meant he was going to get into his camper van and drive away to whatever place he considered his *real* home. Surely, a person couldn't live in a mobile house like that. It wasn't natural.

When Michael had left, her grandfather sighed. "Now, there's a lonely man."

"Lonely? He didn't look lonely to me," Abbie said.

"Well, I can't see him. But he's got the loneliest voice I ever heard."

The evening before Beth's wedding, Abbie and Beth used nut grinders to crush pecans and graham crackers in the kitchen for eight sawdust pies.

"Are you jittery?"

Beth laughed. "I can't wait. Ever since Jacob drove me home from Sunday night singing, I knew it was only a matter of time. Hopefully, we'll have a house of our own by spring."

"Dawdi's English guest asked if he could come to the wedding. I told him that the guest list was full."

"That was rude," Beth commented. "He is staying in the community, he might as well have attended."

"How do you know who he is? And why should we trust him?"

Beth reached out and touched Abbie's shoulder with her sugar-covered hand. "I know you've been hurt by an Englisher before, Abbie, but that doesn't mean they're all like that."

Abbie turned away. "You're getting my frock all sugary."

She didn't want to think about that time she'd been hurt. She never wanted to be fooled like that again.

Wedding vows always made Abbie feel that odd choked-up feeling. She didn't like crying in front of other people. As the bride's sister, she was seated in the front so she made an effort to keep her face stoic and scanned the crowd.

The people were mostly from their church district with some relatives who had travelled in order to be here Suddenly, she gasped as she glimpsed Michael's face in the crowd. He was wearing an Amish hat and the traditional trousers and suspenders. Naturally, he still stood out with his Asian appearance but he didn't seem to care too much.

He'd come anyway. Had he been invited by her grandfather? Abbie figured that was the case. Irritating? Yes, but there was nothing *she* could do.

After the traditional feast and opening of presents, Abbie went upstairs quietly to get her things ready. They were having an elderly aunt stay with them for three days because she had travelled on a long trip in order to be here, so Abbie had agreed to give up her room to the aunt and stay with dawdi instead.

"Abbie, are you all set to go?" her mother asked, peeking in.

"Almost." Abbie turned around. "Did you see the Englisher, mam?"

"I did."

"He shouldn't have come. He wasn't invited."

"He gave your sister a large KJV Family Bible. A good practical gift."

"He did?" Abbie frowned. "If he has the money to give wedding gifts to people he hardly knows, why does he need to live in a van instead of a real house?"

"I don't know. But he seems real interested in the Amish. He asked about a million questions when talking to your cousins. Maybe he'd like to join us. I knew a man to do that once."

"I think he's writing for a newspaper, after all," Abbie said.

She walked downstairs and approached the buggy that was being driven by her cousin Joshua. Michael was standing by the buggy and he offered her his hand to help her in. Abbie hesitated, then took it.

Once they set out, Abbie listened to Michael and Joshua speaking quietly in the front row of the buggy.

"Do you need any help in your shop, Mr. Stratsburger?"

Joshua shook his head. "Honestly Mr...." he hesitated.

"Call me Michael."

"Well, uh, Michael then. I would have to know you for months before I could hire you. I'd have to get a recommendation from your bishop back where you used to live and he would have to be an Amish bishop. I don't hire people from a different faith. That's job ust my preference."

Michael gave a quiet sigh. "I see."

Suddenly, a police car pulled up beside them.

Joshua held the horses back. "Whoa."

The three of them turned to face the police officer, who was just getting out of his car.

Abbie had seen Officer Ron Baker about three or four times in her life when he came to their community meetings. Officer Ron got out of the car and walked towards their buggy. He always slouched when he walked. Abbie wasn't sure if it was because he was so tall or because he had never been taught to stand up straight.

"We've got a bit of a problem," he said. 'Where are your buggy lights?"

Joshua brought his hand up to his forehead. "Oh! They're broken, I forgot to get them fixed."

"You're not so easily visible on the road. You want to get your family killed?" Officer Ron's gaze travelled over the four of them and stopped on Michael. "What's your name?"

Michael cleared his throat. "Uh...Michael. Michael Wong."

Officer Ron rubbed his chin. "Michael. That's interesting. Are you visiting Birchtown?"

"Yes, I'm staying with this gentleman here. Just arrived."

You haven't heard about the bank robbery that happened about a week ago over in Mill City. It was on the local news."

"Which channel?"

"Did you hear about it or *didn't* you?"

Michael swallowed. "Yes, sir, I did. From a friend."

"An Asian man walked into the bank with a stolen ID. Said his name was Michael Chan and had an ID to match. The girl at the front desk hadn't seen too many Asian faces and figured he was the same man that was represented on the picture. She glanced at the ID and let him withdraw $800. Then, a week later, the real Michael Chan called us, saying that he had noticed a withdrawal on his account."

Abbie frowned. "How did he notice it without coming in?"

"I'm guessing he was looking at his account online," Officer Ron said. " You wouldn't know how the internet works, miss, so don't worry about it. Anyway, the bank refunded the money, but we're still looking for the thief. And all we really know about him is that he was Asian, probably Chinese, in his late twenties or early thirties."

Michael smiled uneasily. "There are lots of men that are Asian."

"It's also interesting that your name is Michael."

"Michael was the name of the victim, not the thief."

"Hmmm. You're staying with the Amish. *Why?*"

Michael shrugged. "I needed to get away from home but not too far away, if you known what I mean. I needed to clear my head. I had my camper van. So I came here."

Officer Ron gave him a long, hard look. "I see." He turned back to Joshua. "Now, I'm going to write down your name and address. I'll let you off with a fee this time but better get those buggy lights fixed. Several more infractions and that could be a prison sentence."

After officer Ron drove away, they continued the journey in silence.

Finally Elias broke the silence with "You know where to get those buggy lights, Joshua?"

"Yes, dawdi."

"Good. Get them tomorrow. And I'm thinking it shouldn't be so easy for a person to get money from another man's account. If they've got so many thieves out in the English world, they've got to have better ways of catching them."

"Maybe they will arrest him," Abbie suggested. She wondered why Michael had seemed nervous at seeing Officer Ron. Did he have something to hide?

Chapter Two

Michael woke up before sunrise.

It wasn't typical for him to wake up so early and it occurred to him that the best way to use the hours of the morning was to catch some bass. He'd loved fishing as a child. His father had been a hard, angry man and his mother constantly working, but once or twice a month, his grandfather had taken him to a quiet country brook. Then, they'd sit on the bank, talking a little but mostly, just breathing and thinking.

He glanced at the large, solid Amish house. He'd just peek in quietly before going on. Abbie was probably still sleeping.

He rapped lightly on the door, before opening it.

The kitchen smelled of butter and sugar. Elias was sitting in his usual armchair, sharpening some kind of pencil with his hunting knife. Abbie was making pancakes, her dark braid up in a bun.

"Is that you, Michael?" Stay for the pancakes," Elias offered and Michael allowed himself to be talked into sitting down.

"I'm just here for a minute. I'm all ready to go fishing."

Abbie nodded. Yesterday, she'd glared at him during the wedding but today, she seemed more friendly now that the roles were clearly outlined, she as the hostess and he as guest. "Dawdi used to take me when I was younger. Then, one day, when I was around fourteen, I asked to go and he said, 'Abbie-girl, don't you have some nice embroidery to do'? I guess I was too old to go do a male activity like fishing anymore."

Her grandfather chuckled from his armchair. "My vision was already failing. I figured you might fall into the lake and who would rescue you if I couldn't?"

Michael considered this. "Did you actually enjoy embroidery? Or were you just stuck doing it cause the other women did?"

"Mommi, my grandmother, got me into making tapestries to sell to the families around me. I think I mostly enjoyed earning money. Even if most of it went to my dat, I enjoyed knowing I was bringing money in and counting up how much."

"So you always enjoyed having a business."

"Jah. I was best at mathematics at school. I could add up a bunch of sums faster than you could blink." Abbie finished flipping the pancakes and turned the stove off carefully. "What do you do?"

"I liked working with music back in college. But then I stopped doing that and worked driving a truck for a while. Then I cooked at a Chinese restaurant. I can make the best chicken. Finally, I...well, I think I finally found something I liked. But I've moved on from *that* too."

"What was it?"

Michael considered telling her. She would probably disapprove of his career. He had been a massage therapist for several years and he didn't think the Amish had those. And yet, couldn't everybody benefit from getting a massage on a stressful day?

"It doesn't matter," he finally said. "The fact is it just doesn't seem like I can stick to anything for too long."

Abbie frowned. "That's not the way it should be. A girl can get away with doing a little bit of this and a little bit of that because, in the end, she's supposed to take care of her kids. But a man...you've got to pick one trade and work at it, so you get better." She was suddenly aware that Michael was looking at her ironically, as if she was a child saying something naive. "I mean...why not?"

"People don't always let you get better," Michael said. "Sometimes, you're stuck doing the same exact thing day after day with no skill to it at all. And then, when you finally find a job you enjoy, a job where you can help people and get paid for it, something happens that's out of your control and you're back to the beginning."

Elias cleared his throat. "I don't know much about the English world. But here in our community, hard work and skill are appreciated."

Michael watched Abbie for a moment as she set down the coffee pot, her cheeks red from the exertion.

On an impulse, he offered, "Why don't you come fishing with me?"

Abbie hesitated.

"You've got a fishing line, don't you?"

"Yes. But..."

"If you do fall in the lake, I know how to swim."

Abbie imagined the sun just rising, the clear waters of the brook, the crisp fall air and the smell of the dried leaves... "All right. But I have to be back by 7:30 AM to get home for cleaning up."

As they sat on the bank, their fishing lines extended, Abbie wondered about Officer Ron's visit yesterday. Could it really be so easy to steal from someone? She knew that in their local bank 5 miles from here, it would never work. But that was only because the teller knew nearly every single Amish and non-Amish family by appearance.

Michael broke into her thoughts. "Your sister's wedding yesterday was beautiful."

"Yes, it was."

"I've only been to two weddings in my life."

Abbie stared. "Only two? You don't have too many friends."

Michael laughed. "Where I come from, men don't settle down quite so early. None of my friends have gotten married yet. I was at my mother's second wedding six years ago. I even helped her choose the music for the main dance."

"What's that?"

"The groom and the bride dance with each other while everyone else watches."

Abbie pictured it. It was *different*. But it sounded lovely.

"Do you want to hear the music? It's one of my favorite songs. It's about the first couple in creation." He tapped the screen of his phone a few times. "Just listen to this."

A female voice was singing to the faint strains of a guitar.

"At last, at last, bone of my bone and flesh of my flesh..."

Abbie felt a shiver pass over her. It was somehow similar to the hymns of her childhood and yet, completely different.

"And like the dawn you woke the world inside of me,
You were the brightest shade of sun, when I saw you."

Abbie glanced at Michael, then stared determinedly at the sparkling water. When the song was finished, they sat quietly.

"I liked your sister's ceremony because it was so simple. Simple and true."

It's not a complicated thing, getting married. It's what comes after that is really complicated."

"That's about right. My mother and father…didn't get along. It was mostly my father's fault. He used to hit us kids, he'd hit my mother. Then she'd refuse to speak to him at the next day but she never left him."

Abbie opened her mouth to say, *Marriage is forever.* But the words got stuck on her throat. He *hit* her? *Daily?*

"Children shouldn't be hit too hard," she finally said, falling back on the obvious.

"What about 'spare the rod and spoil the child'?"

"I've seen toddlers spanked by their dats by hand but never with a rod," Abbie said. She shrugged. "But Bishop Hoffman does speak about disciplining children. Just in other ways." Suddenly, Abbie felt the tugging on the line. "I think I got one."

"You did?"

"Yes. Wait." Abbie yanked the fishing like out of the lake and the fish with it. "Ain't it a beauty?"

Michael's eyes lingered on Abbie's face. "Sure is."

Abbie was suddenly aware that she was blushing.

———————————————————-

When Abbie arrived back at her home, Beth and her mother were already hard at work, scrubbing the floors and sorting the leftover food into tupperware containers. Their elderly aunt who had come to visit was reading in the living room.

Abbie got to work but watched Beth carefully.

Beth was quiet. She smiled frequently but said very little. She and Jacob had spent the night in Beth's room and had been allowed to sleep in until 7:00 AM, which was late for a farming family. Her new husband Jacob was off delivering borrowed tables and benches.

As Abbie scooped out some leftover apple dumplings, she found herself humming. "At last, at last..."

"What song is that?" her mother inquired.

Abbie suddenly felt embarrassed, although she wasn't sure why. "Just a song I heard, mam," she said. "It's about Adam and Eve."

"I don't really see how it's about Adam and Eve," her mother said, puzzled. "Their story is about sin."

"I don't think it's only about sin. It's also about love."

Her mother shook her head, laughing. "This wedding's got you talking nonsense."

For dinner, Abbie went back to dawdi's house and cooked up some of the bass Michael had caught along with some baked potatoes. After a day full of cleaning and organizing, she was grateful for an easy dish to cook. This time, it seemed only natural to invite Michael.

After Elias blessed the food and they began to eat, Abbie brought up the bank theft again. Something about it was bothering her, though she couldn't say what.

"Think they'll ever find the man who stole that money?"

"It'd be mighty hard," said Elias.

Michael was quiet.

"What do you think?" Abbie asked him.

He shrugged. "What do I think? Let the cops figure it out. I'm not a cop."

"Do you think there's some way to make sure robberies don't happen?"

Michael considered this. "Some government places, they scan your fingerprints. You know, nobody ever has two alike?"

"I didn't know that."

"Yes. One of the signs that we were made by a creator." He picked up a rag and began to wipe down the table.

Abbie stared. She had never seen a man help with housework.

"You don't have to do that."

"I don't mind. My mother used to say, 'The maid is off duty today, so we all do the chores.'"

"You had a maid?"

"No."

Abbie laughed.

"Next time your dawdi's having chicken, I can cook it and you can come over and eat with us," Michael said. "I make really good chicken. I've got nearly all the ingredients in my camper van." He smiled at her and Abbie could hardly look away.

She had gotten so comfortable that she'd nearly forgotten that Michael Wong was an Englischer. When had she stopped thinking of him as a handsome intruder and started thinking of him as a new friend? Sometime, while they were fishing? Sometime, during dinner?

Once they had cleaned up, Michael rose to leave. Abbie thought of the evening stretching out ahead of her. She *had* brought a tapestry to work on but, after all, if there was fun to be had, why not have fun together?

You're too trusting, she said to herself. *Keep a distance.*

But this was only a friendship.

"Do you want to play something?" she said. "Dawdi's got a few games up in the attic."

Michael's face brightened.

After some discussion, they decided on Clue Junior. It was a children's game, yes. But Michael didn't seem a bit embarrassed by that. It was a logic game that involved eliminating all the wrong answers until you had only one left.

They threw the dice and moved their game pieces around the board, laughing, as they each tried to figure out who stole the pet from the little boy, what kind of pet and at what time of day.

"It was a goldfish, I think," Abbie said finally.

"Why would *anybody* steal a goldfish?" Michael asked.

Abbie laughed. "Why would anybody steal at all?"

Michael looked away. "Sometimes, people do."

"Oh." Abbie stared at him, feeling suddenly chilled. "Have you?"

Michael cleared his throat. "Once. I was in college and I was working in the music section of the bookstore. I stole some CDs. It was foolish decision and I got fired for it. Haven't stolen anything since." He threw the dice, a bit wildly, and it rolled off the table and towards Abbie's feet.

"There ain't nobody perfect on Earth," her grandfather said gently from his armchair in the corner.

Abbie leaned over to pick up the dice. So he had stolen in his past. Maybe her cousin had been right not to hire him.

And yet...didn't everyone deserve another chance?

"I think I'll go fishing again," Michael said. "It's a nice place to fish."

"I want to go into town tomorrow," Abbie said. "I need to take out some books for dawdi at the library. I read to him a couple of nights a week. I also want to buy a photo camera."

"What do you need a camera for?"

"I want to get a catalog made for all of my tapestries. I'll get all the photos done with my camera and then bring them into the catalog store."

"That's not a bad idea." Michael thought for a moment. "Why don't you use my phone to take your photos? I can e-mail all of your photos over in one file. And if anything happens, I'll still have them saved."

"You don't have to pay extra for that?"

Michael laughed. "Oh no. It comes with the phone. But Abbie, I'd have to be with you while you took those photos. I can't be away from my phone. Ever."

"You're waiting for an important call?"

A sorrow seemed to pass over Michael's eyes. "I hope so," he said.

Abbie shrugged. "I don't know. Maybe I should look at camera prices anyway."

"Between that and tomorrow's chores, I don't suppose you've got the time tomorrow to have a cup of hot apple cider with me at the donut shop on the corner of Main Street? Right by the library? It's where you're going anyway, isn't it?"

Abbie's face flushed. The Englischer wanted to ask her out on a date?

"I...I don't know," she muttered, confused. She found herself staring at the floor.

Abbie had been been invited to ride home from Sunday meeting with some of the boys several times this month. Each time, she had refused them hardly knowing why.

"Apple cider might be nice," she said. "But if you pay for the cab, I'm paying for my own apple cider."

After Abbie headed upstairs to sleep, Michael headed to the door but Elias's voice stopped him.

"Come talk to me for a bit, Michael."

Michael came back. "Yes, sir."

"Now," Elias said frankly. "I've met you and I like you. I've heard you look different. I can't tell and I don't care if you look different. But I need to know if you're planning on staying here long."

"Um..." Michael paused. "I'm waiting for an important call on my phone. Then, I will probably be gone for a while. Then I might come back for a bit longer."

"'*A while?' Probably? A bit longer?*' Your answers are all very vague, aren't they?"

"Yes, sir."

"Eventually, you're going to have to decide. If you earn people's trust, you might gradually find work here. But is that what you want to do?"

"I really like your town," Michael said. "If I could set up a business doing what *I'm* good at but set it up here...I'd never want to leave."

Elias frowned a little. "But if you can't, you might have to leave. And until you've decided, you'd better be careful what promises you're making. Abbie's a very sweet girl."

"I wouldn't hurt Abbie."

"I warned you to be careful. The Lord holds us accountable for the people that we form friendships with."

Chapter Three

The next day, Abbie woke and, after a quick breakfast, headed home to do her daily chores. Thursday was ironing day. She and her mother ironed all of Jacob's clothes now, in addition to all the clothes for their family of ten.

Beth seemed a little teary-eyed today. "It's sinking in," she said. "I'm never going back to teaching. I'm just going to sit in the house and wait for baby after baby."

"Didn't you want this?" Abbie asked, puzzled.

"Jah, I did. But it's a big change. And change is painful, even if you're giving something up for something better." Beth smiled. "I don't regret it."

"Even when I get married, I'm not stopping my tapestry work," Abbie said vehemently. "My husband will just have to get used to it."

Beth shook her head. "You'll need to think about what's best for your family, Abbie. You'll need to consider others, before yourself."

In the afternoon, Abbie went upstairs to get ready for her trip into town with Michael.

There wasn't much she could change. She brushed her hair and put on a freshly laundered kapp. She was getting a curious feeling in the pit of her stomach and she laughed at herself. Over a trip to the library and some apple cider?

She headed over to dawdi's house with a cloth bag for library books slung over her shoulder. When she entered the house, she couldn't quite locate him at first.

"Here, Abbie," she heard him call from the next room.

He was sitting in his favorite armchair with his head tilted back and his eyes closed as Michael rubbed his back.

"What are you doing?"

"I've been dealing with some head and neck pain," said dawdi, turning his head slightly. "Could barely sleep last night. Michael said he could do a...what do you call it, a *massage*?"

Abbie had never heard of the word "massage". She could tell that he was just rubbing her grandfather's back to make him feel better. She'd seen women do it for the old folks and sometimes for the children but to see a man doing it...it did look *odd*.

"It's supposed to help with neuralgia," Michael said, his fingers still moving rhythmically. "Want me to show you how?" Michael reached for her hands, took them gently and placed it under his. "If you've ever kneaded dough, you have the strength in your hands to do it. You just need to learn."

Abbie tried for a few minutes but she found herself watching the clock.

Michael noticed. "Are we off?"

"Go Abbie," her grandfather said. "As long as you're back in time to help your dat milk the cows. And Michael?"

"Yes sir?"

"You'd better treat her with respect. There are strong men standing behind her to defend her if anything goes amiss."

"Yes sir."

Michael called a cab to get them to the library. Abbie had been in a cab several times but, to her family, it was still a rare thing.

As they sat in the car, Michael tried not to stare at the way Abbie's brown hair peeked out from underneath her kapp.

"Do you ever get books for yourself?"

"If I did, mam would want to look over them first. To make sure I'm not reading anything indecent. That makes most adult books inappropriate and I've grown out of *Tom Sawyer* and *Pollyanna*."

As they approached the front desk, Michael took out his library card and addressed the librarian. "Ma'am, get this young lady a book full of stories by O.Henry. She doesn't know what she's missing."

Smiling, Abbie looked down and her gaze fell on the library card.

The name imprinted on it made her freeze.

It said *Michael Chan*.

The world spun briefly around her and then stopped spinning.

"I'll need your ID as well if you want to check the book out," the librarian said to Michael.

Michael sighed and pulled it out.The name on it was *Michael Chan* as well.

Abbie leaned against the desk.

The librarian handed her the book.

"Thank you," Abbie muttered.

"Did you want to look around?" Michael asked.

"Yes, look around," Abbie repeated.

"All right then. Guess I'll be over in the history section."

As soon as Michael had stepped away, Abbie sank into a soft armchair positioned by one of the library shelves and tried to think.

Either he was really named Michael Chan and had taken advantage of having the same name by stealing another man's money *or* he was *not* Michael Chan at all but had Michael Chan's identification. In any case, he had called himself Michael Wong, which meant that he'd lied to Officer Ron about his last name. And had lied to her.

Just as she had been lied to once before.

No wonder he had seemed nervous. No wonder he has not really wanted to discuss the case with her.

Abbie knew that she ought to go and select some books for dawdi but she couldn't bear to get out of her seat. She could just sit there, trying not to burst into hysterical tears. Angry as she was, she needed to wait for Michael and they would need to share the cab ride home.

Right after that, she would call Officer Ron from the community phone booth.

It took until they had left the library for Michael to realize that something was wrong.

"Why don't you want to get apple cider?"

"I just don't," Abbie said quietly. "We must be getting back."

"Abbie, did something happen while I was gone?"

He looked at her, sorrowful and puzzled, and Abbie felt an urge to strike him on the shoulder with her fist.

"Please call a cab."

"I'm not calling anybody until I understand what's wrong."

'You're not letting me get *home*?"

Michael handed his phone over. "Here. Call. I certainly don't want to keep you trapped here in town against your will."

He stood by while Abbie called. "I saw your library card," she said, once the call was finished. "And I saw your real name."

His lips parted a little.

"You are the thief that officer Ron was looking for. You lied to me and you lied to all of us."

Michael reached for Abbie's hand, gently, but Abbie yanked it away. "Well, *didn't* you?"

"I didn't steal that money."

"I don't believe you."

"Abbie, I *did* lie about my name. My name *is* actually Michael Chan. But I didn't steal the money. Somebody came in and impersonated a Michael Chan at the bank and I just happen to have the same name. So when the police officer came with his announcement here, I decided to lie about my name so that nobody would suspect me."

"Prove it to me."

"I *can't*. But Abbie, my name is just...an unlucky coincidence that's all. Do you know how many Michael Chans there are in the USA? You have common names among the Amish. You know that several Asian people can have the same name too. Abbie, don't cry. It's just a misunderstanding."

"You *still* lied to me," Abbie said. "I was beginning to respect you, respect you so much that I was thinking of you in my mind as a very, *very* good friend and, now, I can't anymore, it's all *spoiled*."

Michael winced. "Spoiled? What about forgiveness?"

"I had an Englischer man become my friend once. I was working at a grocery store and he was doing deliveries. He borrowed money from me *promising* to give it back the next day and then, he disappeared. And forgiveness isn't forgetting."

" I'm sorry you've been through that."

"This isn't about me. This is about you. You're dishonest about who you are."

"I couldn't take the risk of giving Officer Ron my whole name. I can't post bail and I can't spend even a few nights in jail while they straighten things out, I've got to be available. I've got someone depending on me."

Abbie turned away. "I don't even know if I should believe you about *that*."

""Look," Michael pulled out his wallet. "This is my sister."

He showed Abbie a picture of a pretty young girl in her twenties with almond eyes and a slim build. She was standing next to a tall, muscular man in a baseball hat.

"My sister lives in Mill City. She moved in with this man about 7 months ago. He hits her, Abbie. Hits her and criticizes her all the time, just as my father did, but she wants to stay with him anyway. I tried talking to her but it's her decision and I can't stop her."

"They look happy," Abbie muttered.

"Yes, well..." Michael stuffed the picture back in his wallet. "I've got to stay near. I have a feeling someday she will have had enough. Then she'll call me. There isn't anybody else to call."

"Do you mean she'll need you to come and take her into your home?"

"Oh no. I'll help her move out, set up her own furniture, help her start living on her own. She's got a different way of living from mine and she wants...privacy. But I would be glad for her if she could just leave this screwball and start over."

"And you thought that being sent to jail might happen on the same day as a call from her?"

Michael spoke heatedly. "I've been prone to too many unlucky coincidences lately. They reduced my hours at work just two weeks ago which meant that I couldn't keep affording the rent for my apartment unless I found another job. But I already owned the camper van. So I moved into it and left everything behind. Your community seemed like a peaceful place to stay while applying for work. And then when I saw the land and met the people, I wasn't sure I ever wanted to leave."

Abbie studied him again. The information about his sister she had believed right away. Clearly, he loved her. But this didn't mean he couldn't *also* be a bank robber. He had just admitted that he was desperate for money.

"It would be very easy for you to use *your* ID for the other Michael's account."

"Not really. I don't use that bank. I would somehow have to know that there *was* a Michael Chan registered there. And I'd have to know that he had money on his account. I can't *make* you believe me, Abbie. I can only ask you to."

Abbie glanced at the sky. It was still light. She had three hours before she had to be home to help with feeding the animals and mucking out the stalls. "Let's go over to the bank in Mill City then," she said. "If the girl working there really doesn't think you did it, she won't be able to recognize you. If she does recognize you, then I'll know for sure."

Michael thought it over. From his point of view, the plan made sense. Of course, Abbie had clearly not read too many mystery novels. To go on an investigative journey along with the *one* person you suspect of being the criminal...it was almost funny but he couldn't laugh. He had seen the feeling of betrayal in Abbie's eyes and wanted to fix it. He had never meant to hurt her but had managed to do that very thing.

Chapter Four

The city bank was a three story building, much taller than the bank Abbie's family used to keep their savings. When Michael asked the teller if she knew the girl who had been on duty on the night of the burglary, the teller responded, "And why would you need that information, sir?"

"It's...it's complicated," Michael said. "But you see, I'm trying to prove to my friend that I...never stole any money. And she thinks I did because I look Chinese and the thief was too and...if we could just talk to her for a moment, I'd be able to prove my point."

Abbie took a deep breath and kept her temper. The way he had summarized it made her appear to be a complete idiot. But she didn't go as far as pointing out his *name* to the teller. Until she was sure, she would keep him from getting into trouble.

The woman smiled finally. "Hey, Alexis!" she called. "Would you come over for a moment?"

Alexis came walking up to the desk. She was slightly overweight with brown hair with light brown highlights and looked at the two of them, quizzically.

"Is this the guy who tricked you the other day into withdrawing money from Mr. Chan?"

Alexis looked over Michael carefully. "No."

Michael turned to Abbie. "See?"

Abbie wasn't satisfied. "How do you think the man got Mr. Chan's ID?"

Alexis shrugged. "I'm not sure. Guess he lost it and the thief found it. Or maybe he stole it. I heard Mr. Chan didn't even know his ID was missing until he saw that the money was missing from his online account. We should install fingerprint machines."

Abbie persisted. "But didn't they also need to give some kind of code?"

"If a person forgets their debit card, usually a photo ID is enough," said the other teller. "You know that Mr. Chan, he's kind of an absent-minded man. Didn't he leave behind his whole wallet like a month ago? Then he came back for it but it was sitting on this desk for a good part of the day."

Alexis shook her head. "I don't remember."

"You never remember anything." The teller turned back to them. "Can I help you with anything else?"

Michael shook his head. "I don't use this bank."

Abbie blushed a little as she also shook her head. She still kept her money combined with her parents' on their account.

They walked out of the bank.

"All right," Abbie said. "I believe you. But you've got to see why I got so angry. When I was sixteen, I was meeting with a boy and he and I became good friends. He borrowed some money from me and it was months before I heard from him again. And when he *did* contact me, he admitted that he had been avoiding me on purpose".

"I never meant to make you feel deceived."

"Well, you still did," Abbie said.

"I'm sorry for that," Michael said. It had become clear to him that Abbie wasn't going to just forget the incident. She has changed in her manner towards him, had gone back to speaking in the cautious, polite tone she had had with him when she'd first met him.

He had liked spending time with her yesterday, had enjoyed fishing with her, talking to her, explaining a thing or two, enjoyed it so much that it almost scared him. You weren't supposed to grow infatuated with someone so quickly. It was supposed to take weeks or months, not one day.

He began to talk to fill up the silence.

"When you've got time, you've got to read O. Henry. Some of his stories are very sad but they're...insightful. People have so many different ways of living, Abbie. You've never gotten to see it."

"I think our way of living is fine," Abbie said icily.

Maybe, Michael thought sadly, a little distance between them was for the best. After all where could a relationship like theirs go?

At least, he could help her with something that nobody else could. "I know you don't feel like apple cider right now," he said " But since we're in the city, do you want to buy a camera?"

They came out of the camera store, Abbie holding her new camera gingerly. It was $100 dollars, and had something called a wifi connection, which Michael said would help Abbie out once she was actually going to see the man who made catalogs.

Abbie kept running her fingers over the shiny black surface of the camera. She realized that she liked owning something this fancy. She liked that it was hers.

"If you need any help figuring out how to use it, I'm right over by your grandfather. Ask me anytime," Michael said.

Suddenly, there was a melody, bells jingling a simple tune.

Abbie looked around but Michael had snatched up his phone. "Hello? Liz?" His face was suddenly full of concern that was almost painful to watch.

"Yes? All right, I can come. Where are you staying? All right."

He tapped on the off button and looked back at Abbie. "It's my sister. She's decided to stay at a hotel room while she's finding a new home."

Abbie tried to understand. "Doesn't she have a mother? Or would she not take her in?"

Michael smiled a little. "My mother lives 8 hours from here."

"So far?" Abbie couldn't imagine being so far from her family.

"I'll need to stay in Mill City for a while. I'll help Liz move, make sure that the man she's leaving knows his place. I hardly see the point to going back to my van at all." He considered for a moment. "Let me get you a cab."

This was all happening much too fast for Abbie.

"But you're just going to go off and leave your things behind? Where will you be staying?"

Michael thought. "Here's my number. I can't give you an address, I don't know where we'll be staying. But I'd like to keep talking to you, Abbie." His eyes lingered on her face for a moment.

"I won't be able to call," Abbie explained. "We only use the community phone for emergencies."

Michael looked away. "The timing is awful. I didn't want to leave today! But Liz needs me."

He really was leaving.

Abbie had a strong sense that this was forever, that if he *did* come back, it would only be to get his camper van. He had a part time job in Mill City (which was better than nothing) and a sister. Why had he come to stay with the Amish in the first place?

Something else occurred to her. "Tell me honestly," she said. "Did you initially come to the Amish community to hide from the police *because* of that whole mix up with your name?"

Michael winced. "Well...mostly, yes. I'd heard about the story and heard the name and because it was the same as mine, I wanted to avoid trouble."

"So once they sort it out, you will have no reason to hide anymore."

"That's true."

Abbie looked away. "I hope it all works out for you. May Got bless the rest of your life."

"Abbie, we will meet again."

"It's possible. Good-bye, Michael." She got into the cab.

By the time Abbie had gotten home, she composed herself enough to speak with dawdi. He was blind. He wouldn't be able to tell she had been crying from her voice alone. And although she had always shared everything with him, she wanted to keep this to herself.

Chapter Five

For the next ten days, Abbie did chores, explored the features on her camera and read O.Henry's stories.

She knew that the point of her camera was to take photos of her tapestries only but she found herself snapping pictures of the sunset, pictures of her grandfather's dog, pictures of the food on their table. She avoided only taking pictures of people because she knew it would attract too much attention.

When she visited dawdi, she tried not to look at the white van.

Ten days later, the Statsburger family was having pumpkin soup together.

"We'll be planting winter wheat soon," Abbie's dat said. "I'll be needing you to pitch in more with the animals, Abbie, while the planting's going on. You might as well if you're not going to be taking that teaching job."

"All right," Abbie said. "Listen to this. I've just read a story by O. Henry. It's about a girl who is very sick. She keeps looking out her window at the leaves and she tells herself that when the last leaf falls off the branch, she's going to die. There's a terrible storm. But the leaf just stays there."

Beth thought for a minute. "Did Got make it stay?"

"No, a man painted a picture of a leaf and put it up in the window. She was looking at the picture and because the leaf stayed there, she stayed alive."

"Well, it's only a story," Jacob said. "In real life, only Got decides if you live or die. We can only accept his will."

"Yes, of course," said Abbie. "But sometimes, if we make a decision, that decision makes a difference."

"Decisions are important, yes," her mam agreed. "Where's this girl's family in the story?"

"She's staying with a friend," Abbie explained. "Her family isn't mentioned."

"She's so ill, she might die and her family isn't mentioned?" Mam shook her head. "How the English see the world! I'll never understand it."

When they were clearing the table, Abbie said, "Jacob. Would you bring me an English newspaper again when you drive in from town tomorrow?"

Every day, she had been checking to see if there was anything about the robbery at the bank. So far, there had been nothing.

"Not much in there worth reading," mam said. "Most of it is either about politics or sin."

"I like reading about politics," Jacob said mildly. "Not that I understand all of it. But I think voting is a privilege and I want to know a little about who I'm voting for."

"Well, for a man, maybe," mam said. "I don't get much into it myself." She turned back to drying the dishes.

"I'll get you a newspaper, Abbie."

Abbie's dat looked up. "Oh…Abbie? Bishop Hoffman told me to pass a message along to you. He wants you to come see him later today at his home."

"See him?" Abbie frowned a little. "Why?"

"I don't know, Abbie. Maybe he's heard about your camera. You must admit it's mighty unusual."

Abbie considered asking the bishop if he wouldn't rather meet with her at her grandfather's house. But it seemed much too presumptuous. She dressed neatly, perhaps more neatly than usual and headed for the bishop's house.

Bishop Hoffman was seated at a large desk. His wife, Mary Hoffman was seated beside him and she smiled warmly at Abbie as she took her seat.

"How are you tapestries, Abbie?" asked Bishop Hoffman. "Coming along nicely?"

Abbie nodded. "Would you like to buy one? I'll have a catalog soon with bright colored pictures. I'll mail you a copy."

"That's what I meant to speak with you about, Abbie. We'll be taking a look at a certain scripture." Bishop Hoffman opened his Bible and the read the words, "Do not be conformed to the ways of the world…" He paused and looked at her. "Have you perhaps considered that I might be speaking to you about the camera everyone says you've been using?"

Abbie felt her face heating up. "It's for my business," she explained. "I'm using it to take pictures for my catalog."

"But you're finished with taking those pictures," Mary Hoffman pointed out. "Ain't it so?"

"I still need to keep the pictures. I might need them again. Or I might add more designs to the mix and need to take more pictures"

"Well, our ways wouldn't mean anything if there wasn't some sacrifice involved," Bishop Hoffman said. "Now I can't command you to do anything. You haven't been baptized into the church yet. But I *strongly* urge you to get rid of the camera immediately."

"But if I need it..."

"Now why would you need it? Surely, the variety of tapestries you've already made pictures for is more than enough for a young girl hoping to make a little spending money."

Abbie stood. "All right. I'll think about it."

"This summer, when you're baptized, Abbie, you'll be asked if you still have a camera and you'll need to answer truthfully."

Abbie was already moving toward the door. "This summer, I will answer truthfully." Then, she was running towards dawdi's home, running as fast as she could.

She was breathless,by the time she'd reached his house, and she ignored Blackie's barking completely, as she tapped on the door. She needed to talk to him. She needed some advice.

Nobody answered.

Abbie tapped again, more forcefully this time.

Finally, she entered. Only then, it occurred to her that dawdi was, in all likelihood, asleep. It was only 8PM but dawdi retired early.

Abbie tiptoed upstairs and peeked into dawdi's room. He was laying on his back, snoring softly.

She walked back downstairs

Now what? She couldn't spend the night. Her parents didn't know where she was. And she just couldn't bear to go back yet. Dat and mam would want to know how the meeting had gone. So would Beth. She couldn't lie to them. Or could she? What if she told them that the bishop had simply asked for a confirmation regarding her baptism this summer?

She had always been the kind of person who told her family the truth about everything but she'd never had a reason to lie before.

Was that how Michael had felt during that whole mix-up with his name?

Blackie sat just outside the house, barking and whimpering.

She went back outside to give him a pat. Just as she was kneeling, she heard a voice say, "Hey, there, boy!"

She glanced up.

"Michael!"

Michael had just opened the door of his camper van and now, stood, staring. "Hi, Abbie."

Abbie leaned against the wall of the house. "How long have you been back?"

"A couple of days. How are you, Abbie?"

He had been back for a couple of days. And he didn't let her know. Why? Abbie tried to shrug it off.

"I'm...all right. Bishop Hoffman just had a talk with me and I wanted to talk it over with dawdi."

Michael looked concerned. "Do you think maybe I'll do instead?"

He invited her into his camper van and Abbie hesitated. Was it a car or a house? What were the rules for coming into a man's camper van with nobody else inside?

Yet, something in her was so miffed at being reprimanded by the bishop that she almost wanted to rebel again in some small way. She walked in and sat on the small couch. There was a laptop set up on a small cabinet in front of it. Michael sat down on the couch as well, leaving some space in between the two of them.

"Bishop Hoffman says I'm supposed to get rid of my camera," Abbie said. "It's not enough that I will keep it in a drawer at home and take it out once a year to update my photos. I have to throw it out completely. And when I am baptized in spring, Bishop Hoffman will ask me if I've gotten rid of it."

"You could keep the memory card instead," Michael said lightly. "It holds the photos, remember?"

"Oh!" Abbie gasped. "That's perfect! I won't have to lie at all and I can still keep my photos and, Michael, you've just given me a clever solution!"

Michael looked at her in silence for a minute. "I don't think so," he said, serious now. "I think it would be kind of similar to the way I gave you the wrong last name."

"How?"

"I was making matters simpler for you and, for myself, but it was still a lie. Bishop Hoffman will want to hear that you've truly separated yourself from the world, not found a loophole to his rules."

"But they're foolish rules! Bishop Hoffman goes into town once a year to see an English accountant and the *accountant* has a computer. So, isn't it the same thing?"

Michael shook his head. "You *did* grow up Amish, Abbie? You don't act Amish at all."

"I never tried to start something new before. I just did what I was *told*. Now, that I'm trying to get a business going, I don't really like someone stopping me. And why shouldn't it be *my* affair if I have a cell phone at home? Why should people even know?"

"You don't have to stay here if you don't like the rules, you know."

Abbie stared. "It's not so simple to just *leave*. I love my family. I love the conversations we have every day and the warmth that we feel when we're together in the house getting things done. If I ever left the Amish, they'd never understand. Maybe Got would. But *they* wouldn't."

"No. But you're being faced with a choice about who *you* want to be. Bishop Hoffman, right or wrong, is true to what he says and what he believes. He doesn't pretend, Abbie. I've been wondering ever since I came back who I really wanted to be. But I felt that it would have to be all or nothing, you know? Either completely Amish or not Amish at all. Not *playing* at it. And I kept thinking about you while I was wondering because I like you, Abbie. I really, really do."

"I really like you too," Abbie whispered. A part of her was terrified of admitting it, like saying it would cause Michael to gain some kind of power over her, where he could hurt her so easily...but it was too obvious to hide.

"But I've decided that becoming Amish wasn't for me. Mennonite, maybe. I've been looking into that. It's a completely different type of life from Amish. But whatever I become, I will take it seriously. And you've got to take whatever you choose seriously. If you choose to be baptized into the church, you shouldn't be making up your own rules and hoping that nobody catches you."

Abbie sighed. Michael was so near. She realized that she'd missed him. Hesitantly, she leaned on his shoulder. "I don't want to sneak around. I think I'll just leave my camera at the catalog maker's office and ask him to keep it for me. But after I'm baptized, I won't even be able to get a temporary camera. Not even for a day. I'd be shunned for disobedience. That's just our way."

Michael pulled away, forcing Abbie to sit upright. "It's because I don't want to become Amish that I didn't want to confuse you. I was going to come back for my van and leave without even seeing you. To make it easier for you."

"But...then, why did you tell me you like me *now if* you don't want to court me?" Abbie asked. "That just makes it harder."

"If you considered leaving the Amish faith, I'd court you. Otherwise, it's just a path to heartbreak for both of us."

Abbie sat silent. Even in her anger at the Bishop, leaving had never crossed her mind.

"Isn't there some way I could *try* not being Amish, the way *you* tried living with us for a while? Just to see what it's like?"

"Of course, there is. I'd even help you out. But I couldn't do it *all* for you, Abbie. You'll need your own plan for how you'd live."

Abbie looked at him, studying his intelligent, serious face and thought, nobody she knew had such a way of making her see the world differently. Nobody. Nobody had such a way of making her think.

"I'll have to work it out somehow," Abbie said. "Will you still be here in the morning?"

"I'd like to be."

"Then, let's go fishing while we can. Let's go fishing tomorrow. No matter what I decide!"

That night she lay awake, thinking.

She didn't want to disappoint Got and she didn't want to hurt her parents. But she wanted to try something new and maybe that meant leaving the Amish. Maybe that meant spending some time with Michael. And how would she know if she didn't try?

Suddenly, she sat upright. She realized she knew *exactly* what to do next!

When Michael greeted her in the morning, she didn't even say hello but went right into explaining her plan. "I think I'll take the job teaching at the school around here, after all. See, I didn't want to take it earlier but I didn't really need money for *myself*. Now I do. Dat will let me keep most of my salary if I tell him I'm saving it for my future. Then, come next summer, I will get an apartment somewhere in Mill City, like all those girls in the O.Henry stories. They're always getting apartments and jobs. And I'll still keep selling my tapestries too, I'll have some money coming in from that."

It occurred to her that dat would never let her keep the money if she told him *what* she was saving it for. So she'd have to be secretive no matter which way she chose.

She kept talking. "If I save up some first, I'll be able to live with the English for a while and then, I'll get to decide if I like it or not. I can still come back. As long as I haven't been baptized yet, I can still come back."

Michael stood. "Abbie, I know you've just met me two weeks ago. But if you think there's a possibility that we can meet as two Englishers, as you call them, that would make me happy. I want to show you movies. And take you to the ice-skating rink. But tonight, I have to go back to Mill City. I'm working part-time as a massage therapist and part-time as a waiter at a cafe. But we can write letters. We can keep writing letters all year long."

Abbie paused. "Are there a lot of girls at the cafe where you'll be working?"

Michael smiled. "None of them so enterprising, and brave, and pretty. And none of them has ever dragged me to a bank to make me prove that I'm not a bank robber. I think you've got nothing to worry about."

"Oh, the bank!" Abbie reached into her bag and pulled out a newspaper. "Jacob brought this to me this morning. They caught the thief! It turns out that she was stealing, the girl who was working there. She stole money from the man's account and then made up the whole story about a fake ID."

"So I'm cleared of suspicion."

"Completely."

"I knew it wasn't you. I just wanted to learn how the story ended."

Michael took Abbie's hand. Together they walked towards the brook.

And the words of the song about Adam and Eve came to her again.

Yes, I was waiting in the darkness when I saw you.

bonus : "ABIGAIL'S DILEMMA"

Abigail Esh watched as the familiar hills and plains of her small Pennsylvania community fell into view. It had been a long buggy ride; they had been travelling for half a day.

She felt a small stab of excitement, at the thought of finally coming home. She had been staying with some friends of her family, who were English, for the past month. It was all part of her *rumspringa*. She had sampled many things in the big city, including going to art galleries and English restaurants. It had been enjoyable, of course, and she wouldn't change the experience for the world.

But she wanted to return to her community, and start life as a fully committed adult Amish. She was ready.

At last. Her family's farmhouse was in view.

As the buggy pulled up, her eyes took in every detail: the old ramshackle farmhouse, the outbuildings and hen house. Home.

The front door opened, and her mother was down the veranda steps. Her eyes were shining in excitement.

"Abigail! We thought you'd never get here," she remarked.

Abigail stepped down from the buggy, embracing her mother. It felt like she hadn't seen her in years.

"Mammi! It is so good to be home," she said. "Where is everybody?"

Mrs Esh smiled, a bit indulgently. "Daughter of mine, have you forgotten the routine already?" They walked up the steps to the house, arm in arm. "Your father and brothers are in the fields, of course. They will return for lunch, as is always the way. Your sisters are quilting, over at Mrs Troyer's, as they do every Tuesday."

Abigail flung herself onto the living room sofa as soon as they entered. "It was such a long trip, Mammi. I feel black and blue all over."

"How are the Carlisles?" Mrs Esh walked to the kitchen as she spoke, getting the coffee she had just made and two cups.

"Very good." Abigail sat up, rubbing her eyes. "They send their best wishes. It was a bit of a whirlwind, staying with them."

"I could imagine." Mrs Esh poured the coffee. "Come, have your coffee. It will revitalise you."

Abigail did as her mother requested, walking to the table.

Suddenly, she stopped. She could see the figure of a man at the front door – tall, dressed in the traditional Amish clothing. He had taken his hat off.

Who was he? She had never seen him before. And her eyes seemed to be unaccustomed to the Amish dress. She had been so used to seeing English clothes that it stood out to her. Well, she would get used to it, again, of course.

"Mammi." Abigail gestured toward the door. "Someone is here."

Mrs Esh rose, approaching the door. "Oh, it is only Nicholas! He is helping your father and brothers; he has been here about two weeks, from another county." She opened the door. "Nicholas! What can I do for you?"

The young man smiled shyly, looking from Mrs Esh to Abigail. "I am sorry to disturb you, Mrs Esh. Your husband sent me to tell you not to prepare lunch today, as we are planning to work through."

"Work through?" Mrs Esh frowned. "Stay for a moment, Nicholas. I will prepare something quickly for you all to eat, which you can take back with you. You can't all work from dawn to sundown without food in your bellies. Please, come in and sit down while I get something ready."

Nicholas hesitated, then walked through the door.

"Abigail," Mrs Esh said, "Could you please pour Nicholas a coffee, while I get the food ready."

"Of course, Mammi," said Abigail, glancing sideways at the handsome, shy young man. Who was he? Why was he working here?

"I'm Abigail," she said. "Please, sit down."

The young man did as he was told. Abigail poured him a coffee, then sat down beside him.

"How did you come to work with us?" she asked, taking a sip of her own drink.

"I was looking for some short term work," Nicholas replied, blushing slightly. "I am on my *rumspringa*, and wanted to experience life outside my community for a bit. My father knows yours, from many years ago, and got in contact." He paused, staring at her. "I'm sorry, but you are Abigail, who has been on your own *rumspringa*?"

"*Ja*," Abigail agreed. "I have only just returned, after staying with some English friends in the city."

"Did you have a good time?"

"I did," Abigail said. She looked at his hands gripping the coffee cup. Strong, and firm. "But I am happy to be home. The city life is not for me. The Lord has made that very clear."

"I am glad," he said, smiling at her. He had the bluest of eyes, the colour of the sky on a bright summer's day.

Mrs Esh came back in, carrying a paper bag filled with sandwiches. She handed it to Nicholas.

"Please, finish your coffee," she said, as he stood up.

"Thank you Mrs Esh, but I must return to work," he said. "And thank you for the food. I am sure we will all appreciate it."

He smiled at Abigail, ducking his head. Then he left.

Abigail stared after him, sipping her coffee thoughtfully.

What a handsome young man. And such polite manners.

It was good to be home, for a lot of reasons. And it seemed that there was one more good reason, although Abigail hadn't realised when she had walked through the door.

The day was full of surprises.

***

Now that she was home, it seemed like she had never left. It was funny, how life worked in that way.

She had already been home a week, and was back into the old routine. And the most exciting thing of all was that Nicholas, the shy young man who was helping her family with the harvest, had asked her out on a date.

She didn't know where they were going, as she excitedly got herself ready on Saturday night. But she knew that Nicholas would take her somewhere appropriate, as well as fun. They had just clicked, right from the moment that she had laid eyes on him at the front door.

But he was shy. She had found many reasons to go and disturb her family as they worked, sometimes bringing snacks or drinks. Her brothers would grin at her – they knew what she was up to. She didn't usually come to visit them so often. It had worked. Eventually, Nicholas had asked her out.

Now they sat in Stoll's restaurant in town, having just finished a hearty meal and laughing over a coffee.

Abigail had never been able to speak so easily to a boy. It was like they couldn't keep up with everything they wanted to say to each other. She felt a glow within her, as she looked at him.

They were just thinking of leaving when the door to the restaurant opened. Abigail turned to look automatically. Then wished she hadn't.

Oh, no. It was Christian Raber. She swivelled quickly in her seat, staring straight ahead. Her heart had started to thump uncomfortably. Maybe, if she was lucky, he hadn't seen her.

But her luck wasn't in. She heard his footsteps behind, approaching their table.

"Abigail." He wasn't smiling. "I didn't know that you were back in town."

She turned and looked at him, a bit fearfully. "Just a week," she said, quickly.

Nicholas was looking from Abigail to Christian. He seemed perplexed.

"I am Christian Raber," the man said, extending a hand toward Nicholas. "Abigail has lost her manners, it seems."

Nicholas took the man's hand, shaking it. He looked at Abigail. "And I am Nicholas Fisher."

She stood up, quickly. "We were just leaving, Christian," she said, walking toward the door. Nicholas' eyes widened, but he stood up, too, almost forgetting his hat on the table as he followed her. He had to go back to get it.

They exited, into the cold night.

Christian stood for a moment, staring after them.

His eyes were cold.

***

"What was that all about?" Nicholas had to run to catch up to Abigail.

She turned, stopping to catch her breath. "I'm sorry," she said. "I know that I appeared rude. But I didn't want to speak to him. He has this idea that he is in love with me, and I have given him no encouragement. Honestly." She blinked back tears, staring up at him.

"What does he do?" Nicholas was frowning, staring down at her.

"Oh, nothing much," said Abigail. She was appalled to find that her hands were shaking. Stop it, she told herself. "He is always polite. He just doesn't seem to understand that I am not interested."

She paused, shaking her head slightly. "I have told him enough times. But he doesn't seem to understand. When I next see him, at Church or Evening Sing or wherever, he asks me out again, as if he hasn't listened at all."

Nicholas assisted her up into the buggy. "I am sorry, Abigail. It is hard when someone doesn't listen to you."

"*Ja*," she agreed. She tried to shake the image of Christian, in the restaurant, out of her mind. She was on a date, with Nicholas. Handsome, caring Nicholas.

"Don't worry about it," she said. "I am sure he will realise, eventually."

They rode off, into the night.

They didn't look back. If they had, they might have seen the figure of Christian, standing in the dark street, staring after the buggy long after it had disappeared.

***

"He was in Stoll's Restaurant, Mamm."

Abigail was having a hot cocoa with her mother after the date. Nicholas had dropped her off half an hour ago.

Mrs Esh frowned. "Don't read anything into it, Abigail," she said. "It might have been just co-incidence. Who knows, maybe he needed to get something from Stoll's."

"At nine-thirty on a Saturday night?" Abigail was frowning, too. "No, I know him of old. He followed me there, I am sure of it."

"He never threatens you, does he?" Her mother looked at her over the brim of the mug.

"No." Abigail shook her head. "He is always polite. It's just a feeling I get. He always seems to be where I go, and he won't stop asking me to date him. I think after the first three negatives, he might get the message that I am simply not interested in him in that way. But he never does."

Mrs Esh stood up. "Time for bed, I think. I will talk to your father about this. We don't want to offend the Raber's, but Christian needs to know that he can't harass you. We will have to think it through carefully, though."

Abigail nodded, bringing her mug to the kitchen sink.

"I almost forgot." Her mother looked at her. "How was the date with Nicholas? We got so caught up talking about Christian."

Abigail smiled broadly. "It was lovely," she beamed. "I think that I really like him, Mamm. Do you think he likes me, too?"

Mrs Esh smiled, her eyes softening as she looked at her lovely daughter. "How could he not, my *lieb*?" she replied. "But I don't know how long he is staying for, Abigail. Your father said that he only needed help for a few weeks, and they are almost up. He lives in the next county."

"That's not so far," said Abigail. "We could write letters."

"So you could," agreed her mother. "But it really is time for bed now, Abigail. We have Church tomorrow, don't forget. And I have to be up very early to cook the goose for the lunch."

Abigail followed her mother up the stairs, preparing for bed. She glanced down at her Bible, thinking whether she should look at it tonight or not. It was very late. But she was still feeling jittery after her encounter with Christian, and felt like she needed some comfort.

Her head was drooping over the good book when she suddenly jolted fully awake. What had disturbed her?

She took her candle, and got out of the bed, walking to her window. She peered out into the darkness, but she could see nothing. She tried to shake the feeling of unease away from her. She was being silly. She should blow out the candle, and climb back into bed.

And yet she stayed, staring out the window. It was complete darkness; not even the moon was out tonight, and a thick blanket of clouds had covered up the stars.

She dropped the curtain, and climbed back into bed.

But the unease didn't leave her. Instead, it invaded her dreams...

She was running.

In motion, she suddenly stopped. She looked down at her feet, willing them to move. But it was like they were frozen in quicksand; the more she tried to dislodge them, the firmer they set. She twisted and turned, in a frantic bid to free herself.

He was coming. She knew he was right behind her.

Suddenly, the quicksand turned to ice. She attempted to run, again. But her feet were sliding over the ice. She stumbled, trying to regain her balance.

She heard a noise behind her, and turned quickly.

It was him. She couldn't see him in the shadows, but she knew.

The ice started cracking underneath her feet. She watched it zig-zag, broken veins across the white surface.

And then she was gone, underneath the ice, plunged into cold, cold water.

She stared up, and saw him looking down at her, coldly...

She sat up in bed, breathing heavily. She could feel sweat sliding down her neck.

This had to stop. She didn't know what Christian's intentions were, but he had to know how much he was scaring her. She didn't think that he would harm her, not really. But he was behaving oddly, and she couldn't deny anymore that it was starting to affect her.

She lay back down, drifting back to sleep. Think happy thoughts, she told herself.

The image of Nicholas filled her mind. His handsome face, concerned for her that night when she had told him about Christian. The way that he had helped her down from the buggy when they had arrived home, holding her hand tenderly so that she wouldn't slip. She had looked into his eyes, and seen kindness. His eyes shone with the purity of his soul.

Nicholas. Was she falling in love with him? But she hardly knew him. It had only been their first date, and they had chatted a handful of times before.

And soon he would leave. Return to his farm in the next county, away from her. His *rumspringa* over, just like hers was.

Would she see him again?

The image of Nicholas was the last thing that she remembered as sleep finally claimed her – this time for the whole night.

***

Abigail yawned, trying to stifle it with her hand discreetly.

It was the next day, and she was tired. It had been late before she had finally drifted off to sleep. She looked around at the familiar faces at the church service, but she hadn't seen him yet.

Nicholas. Her heart leapt as she said his name in her head, over and over.

Where could he be?

She tried to concentrate on the service, but her mind was drifting. Her mother had told her that Nicholas had attended their church service since he had been staying with them. And he himself had said that he would see her there. He had been looking forward to her mother's baked goose with apple and cider gravy for lunch, as well.

She surreptitiously scanned the congregation, again. But then she saw Christian Raber, staring at her from the back row. Shivers coursed through her; her skin crawled like it had been invaded by an army of ants.

She looked to the front, trying to concentrate on the service.

But her eyes, sickeningly, were drawn back to him.

He hadn't stopped staring. But now he added a small smile.

She refused to smile back. It would just encourage him. Silly, she chided herself. Even turning her head to look at him again he would perceive as encouragement.

He had always been an intense boy, ever since they had shared a seat in the one room classroom down the road. She could remember that he often would be alone, kicking a stone in the playground while groups around him played. And when he had friends, it would always be only one person, or two. Usually children who were a bit odd, like himself.

She had never been anything but polite to him, but she had drawn the line at friendship. She just couldn't stomach his intense stares. How he had perceived her politeness as anything other than that was beyond her. And yet he had. He had been asking her out for over six months now.

At first, she had been flattered, despite herself. But then it had got annoying. He simply wouldn't listen to her, when she said no. And then he started turning up everywhere that she went: a visit to the bakery, or when she was perusing stalls at the market. Anywhere.

It was one of the reasons she had gone so far away for *rumspringa*. Abigail wasn't much of a traveller, really. She probably would have stayed closer to home. But she had needed a break from his constant attention.

The service finally finished, and people started socialising. She went up to her mother.

"Where is Nicholas?" she whispered. "I haven't seen him today."

Mrs Esh looked at her. "I'm sorry, I forgot to tell you, Abigail," she said. "Nicholas received a note this morning, about something urgent. He needed to return home immediately. I'm not sure if he will be back, my *lieb*. He was due to finish work soon with us, anyway." She looked at her daughter. "Cheer up! You can still write to each other."

Abigail felt her heart sink. She shouldn't be so disappointed, of course. They had only had one date, and Nicholas had a life of his own, far away.

But she *was* disappointed. She couldn't deny it.

She was staring at the wall of the barn, lost in her own thoughts. She didn't see Christian approach until it was too late.

"Abigail." He bowed, slightly. His cold eyes were assessing her, as always. She often felt he looked at her like something strange he had just discovered on the sole of his shoe.

"Christian, I'm sorry, but now is not a good time," she said, quickly. Why was he always silent when he approached her? If she had some warning, she could have scurried away.

"I hear that the young man you went on a date with last night has left us," he continued, as if she hadn't spoken at all. "Very suddenly. Did you know that Frannie Glick knows him and his family? She was just telling me that he has a fiancée, back home."

Abigail gasped. She shook her head. "No, Christian, I am sure that you are mistaken," she replied. "Nicholas didn't mention anything to me about a fiancée. He is an honourable man."

"Is he?" Christian smiled, coldly. "How well do you really know him, Abigail?"

She frowned. She supposed it was true, to a degree. She had only known Nicholas a week, after all.

But she trusted her instincts. He was a good man, she knew it. He wouldn't have deliberately deceived her about having a fiancée.

"Well, I shall talk to him," she said, turning away. "I really must go, Christian. I have to help my mother with the lunch."

She walked away quickly, ducking amongst people. Hopefully he wouldn't follow her.

Was it true? He had said he had got the information from Frannie Glick. She looked around, but couldn't see her.

She frowned. Oh, well. Frannie would turn up, sooner or later. And then she would ask her, how she had come by this information that Nicholas had a fiancée.

As Christian claimed.

She felt the skin crawling on the back of her neck. She looked around, and, of course, he was staring at her. An upsurge of anger shot through her. Would he ever leave her alone?

***

"He did mention a girl he had been dating..." Mrs Esh frowned, squinting her eyes, trying to remember. "Or was it that they had dated in the past? I'm sorry, Abigail. I simply don't remember. But he never mentioned a fiancée, of that I am sure."

Abigail frowned, too. It wasn't the simple yes or no answer that she was wanting. This was very frustrating.

She didn't have a right to demand an answer of Nicholas. They had made no promises to each other; it had only been one date, after all. But she also felt that he did owe her an answer, because it simply wasn't done to be dating someone behind his fiancée's back, if he had one.

If it was true, she never would have agreed to go out with him. It was as simple as that.

Restless, Abigail stood up. "Do you need me for anything else, Mamm? If not, I might go to my room, study my bible for a while."

Mrs Esh looked at her. "Of course, Abigail," she said. "Just come down to help with supper, that's all I require."

Abigail left, bounding up the stairs.

Mrs Esh watched her go, shaking her head slightly.

Her daughter was in a state, and had been since Nicholas had left so suddenly the day before. Mrs Esh was worried about her. It was unlike Abigail. And what was this business with Christian Raber? Abigail hadn't mentioned it to her until after her date with Nicholas. If it was true, it wasn't good, and they should intervene on her behalf. But what if Abigail was just being fanciful? The Rabers were good friends of theirs. Mrs Esh didn't want to cause conflict without reason.

She frowned, pondering. No, they would do nothing, for now. If Abigail continued to be worried, well, they would do something then.

She sighed. It was hard, being young. Navigating your way into adulthood. She might mention some bible passages that Abigail should study, to try to ease her mind.

***

Abigail finished the letter, signing her name at the bottom thoughtfully.

She had been in two minds about whether to write to Nicholas, but she was so wound up she didn't know what else to do. Even if she didn't send the letter, it had felt good to get her thoughts and feelings out onto paper.

She read back over what she had written. She had tried to not be too intense, but still convey her wish to continue corresponding with him. She hadn't mentioned anything about him having a fiancée, except to implicitly imply that if he was seeing someone where he lived, she would stop communicating with him.

She put the letter in an envelope, and sealed it. She wasn't sure of his address; she would have to ask her mother if she knew it.

She left it on her desk, propped up against her lantern.

It was time to help her mother with supper.

***

Outside the farmhouse, Christian could see Abigail leave her desk. He saw the letter. He could guess who it was to. And he knew how to solve this, as well.

He often watched her. He had found a position, quite hidden. He would come over the back way to the house, through the fields, being careful to avoid her father and her brothers working.

He didn't think that he was doing anything wrong. He had, after all, explained to her that he wanted to take her out. It was his intention to make her his wife. She was hesitant, and had said no, but that didn't unduly concern him. His father had told him that girls sometimes said no when they meant yes. His own mother, apparently, had refused his father a few times before finally agreeing to date him.

She just needed a little bit of persuasion, that was all.

He frowned, thinking of when he had walked into the restaurant and seen her on a date. It simply would not do. No other man was allowed to date his Abigail.

It had been a stroke of luck that Nicholas Fisher's father had suddenly needed him back at home; as soon as he had heard that, he seized the opportunity. Frannie Glick was away on her *rumspringa*, and couldn't contradict his story about a fiancée. Frannie was a friend of his, anyway, and as soon as she was back he would contact her and persuade her to corroborate the story.

He smiled. It was all going to plan. He had to get rid of Nicholas once and for all, discredit him in Abigail's eyes. And then he would be there, to pick up the pieces.

She would finally see that he was the one for her.

***

The letter had been sent. Abigail waited for a response, but none came.

Inside, she fretted a little. It was all so strange. She had thought that she and Nicholas had a real connection. But he wasn't responding to her – did that mean that what Christian said was true? That Nicholas had a fiancée back home, and that she had been a diversion while he was away?

But as the days went by, and no letter came, Abigail had to admit it to herself. Nicholas didn't care.

Oh, well. She went about her chores as normal, and smiled and laughed when she was required to. She let no one see her sorrow. It would get better, in time. Of course, it would. They had only known each other a short time. It wasn't as if it was a deep wound.

She studied her bible. The classic passage from Ecclesiastes 3:4, about there being a time for sorrow as well as joy, comforted her. She knew that life couldn't be good, all the time. You could learn from sorrow, and had to accept that sometimes there was sorrow in life. As surely as the tides ebb and flow on the shore, sorrow and joy would come and go.

So Abigail kept telling herself, as the days drifted into weeks.

***

The women sat around the table, picking up their needles to commence their quilting bee.

Abigail picked up hers with a sigh. It had been three weeks, and she had not received a word from Nicholas. It was time to let it go, put it behind her. They had connected, but he had decided that it wasn't worth pursuing. Or, he did have a fiancée at home, and he had been merely dallying with her. Abigail preferred to think it was the former; she didn't want her last impression to be that he was a dishonourable man.

They heard another buggy pulling up outside the farmhouse. The women looked at each other.

"Are we expecting someone else?" Mrs Esh turned to the women.

Frannie Glick walked through the door, puffing slightly.

"Frannie!" Mrs Mueller put down her needle. "We weren't expecting you! Aren't you supposed to be on your *rumspringa*?"

"*Ja*," answered Frannie, smiling at the group. "I returned yesterday, a few days early. Mammi told me that you were meeting today, and I wanted to catch up with you all."

Frannie took her seat, and started answering questions about her *rumspringa*. She had been staying with cousins in Ohio, and had a wonderful time.

Abigail glanced at her as she worked. She was waiting for the break, so she could ask her about Nicholas. It probably didn't matter, anymore. But she wanted to know.

At last, the women started getting up. One went to the kitchen, to prepare coffee and snacks. Frannie rose, and walked to the window.

"Frannie," Abigail said, walking up to her. "It is nice to have you back. I was just interested to know. Christian Raber was telling me that you know Nicholas Fisher and his family."

"Who?" Frannie looked at her, a puzzled expression on her face. "I don't know any Nicholas Fisher, Abigail. I think you must be mistaken."

"Are you sure?" Abigail frowned. "Christian told me that you knew the family, and that Nicholas had a fiancée back where he lives."

Frannie continued to look at her, bewildered. "I have no idea what you are talking about, Abigail. The only Nicholas I know is Nicholas King, who we went to school with."

"I'm sorry," Abigail said. "I must have misheard him. Thank you, anyway."

She turned around, and walked out of the house. She needed to be alone, for a moment. She needed to think.

She sat down on a seat on the porch, thinking deeply.

Frannie didn't know the Fishers. She had never heard of Nicholas. Which meant one thing: Christian had lied to her. About Frannie knowing them, but also about Nicholas having a fiancée.

She felt herself go cold. This was getting serious.

Christian had always been an annoyance. But now, he was actively interfering in her life.

She didn't know what to do. Just that it had to stop, once and for all. He had no right, and she was going to make sure that he knew it.

****

Abigail dressed carefully for the meeting.

She had spoken to Mrs Raber, asking her could she come over for a visit. There was something she needed to discuss with her and her husband, urgently. She also requested that Christian be there for the meeting.

She didn't tell her mother. She knew that she would be concerned about making waves with the Rabers. It was something she was concerned about, too. But she also knew that it couldn't continue. Christian had to be stopped. And the best way of ensuring that was to enlist his parents. Abigail knew Christian. He was obedient to his parents, and his father ruled him with an iron fist.

And it was something that she felt must do, by herself. She had to stand up for herself, once and for all.

Mrs Raber opened the door, and led her to the kitchen table. Coffee and cakes were there, waiting.

"Oh, you shouldn't have gone to so much trouble," Abigail said. She was sweating, a little, and her hands when she took the coffee cup were shaking. She wasn't looking forward to this.

Mr Raber was already there, looking at her expectantly. And then Christian came into the room.

He didn't look happy. But he sat down at the table. Obviously, his parents had insisted.

"So." Mrs Raber looked at Abigail, expectantly. "What did you need to see us about so urgently, Abigail?"

Abigail cleared her throat. She must be strong, but she was very nervous. It could backfire on her, and the Rabers might evict her from their home, saying that she was lying.

How should she proceed?

"Thank you for seeing me," she stated. "I know you are all busy people. I needed to see you about Christian."

Christian looked at her, his face like thunder. She almost balked, but doggedly continued.

"As you know, Christian and I have known each other a long time," she said. "Since school. I have always liked him as a friend, but lately, Christian has been wanting to court me."

Mr Raber smiled. "Nothing wrong with that."

"No," Abigail continued. "There isn't. But I have told Christian many times that I am not interested in him that way, and he continues to pester me. He doesn't listen to my wishes."

Mrs Raber looked at Christian, anxiously. "Is this true, Christian? Have you been pestering Abigail, when she has clearly said no?"

"She wants to go out with me," Christian blurted. "I know she does! She just needs persuading. Isn't that so, Daed? You always told me that women often don't know their own minds, and need a firm hand."

Mr Raber frowned. "That is not what I meant, Christian. Yes, sometimes a girl takes a bit of wooing. But if a young woman has clearly said no to you, repeatedly, then you must do the honourable thing and accept her decision."

"But...but..." Christian shook his head, colouring. "I know that she loves me, deep down!"

Abigail looked at him, coldly. "That is wrong, Christian," she said. "I don't love you, and never will. I have no desire to hurt you, but you must accept what I say. I don't want to court you. I like you just as a friend." That was a little white lie. She didn't like Christian, at all. But she didn't want to completely destroy his confidence in himself.

"Abigail, your wishes will be respected," said Mr Raber, glaring at his son. "I will make sure of it. Christian will not bother you anymore."

"Thank you," breathed Abigail. She turned to Christian.

"I wish you well, Christian," she said. "I hope that you find the woman that you will marry, one who loves you. But she is not me. I hope we can still be friends. Will you shake my hand?"

She offered her hand across the table to him. He looked at it as if he might refuse, then he grudgingly shook it. Mrs Raber looked relieved.

"I must go," said Abigail, rising. "Thank you all so much for letting me speak, and taking me seriously. It means the world to me."

"God speed, Abigail," Mrs Raber replied. Mr Raber smiled at her.

It was over. Christian would not bother her, again. She knew the Rabers, and that they demanded complete obedience. Christian would not dare to defy them, now that they knew. She would have preferred that he realised by himself, but that might never happen.

She had to protect her life. He had already interfered in her budding relationship with Nicholas. She didn't want him to interfere for a minute longer.

***

Abigail was feeding the hens when a shadow fell across her.

Fear gripped her. Oh, no. It wasn't Christian back – was it?

She looked around. Then gasped. It wasn't Christian who stood there, but another tall man.

It was Nicholas!

She stood up, slowly. She couldn't quite believe that he was here.

He smiled at her, a bit tentatively. "Abigail," he said. "Your mother said that you would be here."

"Here I am," she replied, then could have kicked herself. Couldn't she think of anything better to say?

"Do you want to go inside?" He asked. "I need to talk to you."

She nodded, leading the way out of the hen house.

They sat at the kitchen table, staring awkwardly at each other.

"I thought..."

"I'm sorry..."

They laughed, as they realised they had both spoken at the same time.

"You go," said Nicholas, looking at her as if he had never seen her before in his life. It made her glow.

"I thought that you didn't want to see me again," Abigail said, biting her lip.

"I thought the same," Nicholas replied. "When you didn't answer my letter."

"What letter?" Abigail frowned. "I never received a letter from you. I wrote *you* a letter, which you never replied to!"

Nicholas shook his head, frowning. "I don't understand. I never received a letter from you. But I did send one."

Abigail stared at him, perplexed. Then understanding started to dawn on her face.

"It must have been Christian," she said. "I didn't realise he was going to that level. He must have been monitoring our mail box. Mamm leaves letters we want to send in there for Daed to collect and send when he gets to town."

"Christian?" Nicholas frowned. "That man who has been pestering you?" He paled, and stood up. "This is going too far. I will go around to his house, this minute!"

"Nicholas, sit down," Abigail said. "It's alright. I have spoken to his parents. He won't be bothering me anymore."

"Are you sure?" Nicholas sat down, slowly. "Because if he ever tries again, he will have me to answer to!" Abigail could see a vein throbbing in his temple. He was angry.

"So you care about me?" She looked at him, shyly.

"I do," he replied. "So much so, Abigail, that I travelled here today to speak to you, even though I thought you didn't answer my letter." He paused, looking like he didn't know what to say further.

"I care for you, too, Nicholas," she said, shyly. "Can we begin again? Like before Christian started interfering in our lives. He told me you had a fiancée, back home."

"He what?" Nicholas looked gobsmacked. "That is an outright lie! I would never have asked you out on a date if I had a fiancée. You didn't believe it, did you?"

"I tried not to," Abigail answered. "But when you didn't reply to my letter, I thought the worst. It was Christian, all along."

"We can begin again," Nicholas said, looking at her earnestly. "If you are willing?" He reached for her hand, across the table. "And God willing, of course."

"Nothing would please me more," Abigail replied. She took his hand. Happiness swelled up within her.

Christian was out of their lives. Nicholas cared for her.

The time for joy was upon them.

END

The Painted Lake

79

ABBY BARKER

Emma hadn't missed a sunrise since she was old enough to help Mama with the laundry, with the exception of that day last winter when she woke up with a cold that kept her bedridden. To Emma, the sun peeking over grassy horizon signified the beginning of all things: life, journeys, and the potential that comes with each new day. Waking up after sunrise would be like turning down a message of encouragement from God, which Emma couldn't bear to waste, so she woke every day at the crack of dawn ready to face whatever challenges arose and accept all graces given to her. This was a schedule that she intended to keep for all time.

This morning, though, she almost missed it. The night before she spent tossing around in her bed, sometimes staring at the ceiling, sometimes the wall, but almost never the backs of her own eyelids. She was restless, but careful to move softly as not to wake up her pig-tailed younger sister, Abigail, who would not have to feel this nervousness for another handful of years, if she would even feel it then. If it was up to Emma, she would have been baptized years ago, but Mama insisted that she take some time to "test her faith." But she already knew her faith to be true; in her heart she knew it. That was enough for her, why wasn't it enough for Mama? This was the last thought she had before finally drifting off to sleep just before dawn.

It seemed as if no time had passed when Abigail gently nudged her sister awake just as the sun began its morning assent.

"Emma! Em!" she half-whispered, "It's today. You've got to get ready. You've got to go so you can hurry up and get back to tell me everything! What do you think Auntie Willa is like? You have to drive a car!"

Emma couldn't match her sister's excitement, but Abigail was right about one thing: The sooner she left, the sooner the month in the city she and Mama had agreed on would be over and she could come home.

"Abigail, please!" she snapped, "I hardly got any sleep and I have plenty of time to pack my bag." She wouldn't have to pack much. In her letters, Auntie Willa insisted they would go shopping the moment she got settled in.

"The clothing is part of the experience," wrote Auntie Willa, "you won't need your bonnet in the city!"

Emma frowned as she rolled away from her sister and turned her back on the dawn. She wanted to stay in bed forever, but she'd settle for five more minutes.

***

After completing her morning chores, Emma changed into a simple, but flattering white linen dress she thought was suitable for traveling. She looked at herself in the mirror as she brushed her long, sun-streaked hair, trying to untangle the knots on her head and in her stomach. A furrowed brow shaded her wide, hazel eyes and her dusty pink lips were downturned in a nervous frown. Each stroke of the brush brought her a little comfort, but not much. There was a lot to be nervous about. She had never met Auntie Willa and they had only spoken through letters. Mama, while she couldn't contact Auntie Willa herself, suggested that Emma reach out before she left on rumspringa. If she had to leave her home, Emma thought, she might as well try to stay with a family member while she's away. Even if that family member left on rumspringa herself 19 years ago and was the only one of her friends not to return home.

Since Emma wasn't yet an official member of the church, she was allowed to write to her excommunicated aunt, but she did so begrudgingly and only at her mother's expressed wishes. Emma could tell that Mama missed her sister, which helped assuage her reluctance to reach out. If Mama still cared for her, she couldn't be all bad. Even so, that first letter was tough for Emma to write. It read:

Dear Auntie Willa,

We've never met before but Mama says you're her sister, which makes you my aunt. She says you used to look just like her, but your hair was always wilder. I have many aunts and uncles here at home, but you're the only one who lives in the city. Mama said it would be a good idea to write you even though you're not with the church anymore because I'm eighteen and she wants me to see the English world before I'm baptized. If I had it my way, I'd already be baptized by now but Mama thinks it's important to face temptation, and deny it, before I make my decision. If I already know there's nothing that could tempt me more than the Will of God, why should I bother with rumspringa? You're probably not the right person to ask.

Your niece,

Emma Byler

Emma was surprised by how kind Auntie Willa seemed in her reply. She told Emma how excited she was to hear from her oldest niece and that she missed the family "something fierce." She also said that she agreed with Mama that seeing how the other half lives, especially if Emma was going to choose to stay with the church, was incredibly important. The way she said "if" put Emma on edge, but she couldn't help but like her aunt after reading the rest of the letter. Auntie Willa wrote enthusiastically and earnestly, offering up personal details about herself (she had an apartment in Chicago with a collie-mix named Charlie), and ended almost every other sentence with an exclamation point. Eventually, Auntie Willa asked Emma to come stay with her for a while.

Emma instinctively put the brush back on the vanity in front of her before remembering the open suitcase next to her. She picked the brush back up and packed it away. Auntie Willa was already on her way. She offered to drive down from Chicago to pick Emma up since no one in her family owned a car, and their horse and buggy wouldn't be able to make the journey to the city. In her letters, Auntie Willa kept referring to it as a "road trip" in an attempt to make the long ride sound more fun, but Emma had never been farther from home than the next town over and the idea of sitting in a car, another thing she had never done, for hours on end was daunting. Just as she zipped up her bag she heard the sound of Auntie Willa's car pulling up to the house. She sat on her bed with the bag in her lap for a few minutes before meeting her aunt in person for the first time.

When Emma finally walked into her family's kitchen, Auntie Willa was sitting at the table with a cup of water that Abigail brought her. She was wearing a bright red t-shirt tucked into a bright, floral-print skirt that brushed her ankles. Her curly, chestnut hair had apparently never lost it's wildness, but was clipped back in a twist that made it look like the strands were trying to escape. She and Emma had the same eyes, which were staring happily at her from across the room. Mama couldn't see any of this while she stood at the sink washing dishes and her back turned to Auntie Willa.

"Emma!" she yelled, jumping out of her chair and almost knocking over the water, "Emma, I'm so frickin' excited to finally see your pretty face!"

Mama bristled and Abigail stifled a laugh at Auntie Willa's objectionable language. Emma just stood stock-still as Auntie Willa rounded the kitchen table, arms outstretched like a bird taking flight, and encircled her in an enthusiastic hug.

"Emma, we're going to have so much fun. I mean, of course you're going to be doing some very valuable thinking and learning, too," she shot a careful glance at her sister, "but that doesn't mean it won't also be tons of fun!"

This made Mama briskly dry her hands on her apron, step away from the sink and pivot towards the hugging pair.

"Now you listen, Willa. Emma is staying with you because I think it's a necessary part of a young person's life to look the world straight in the eyes, knowing everything they need to know about their choice, and say 'My priorities lie with God.' It's not about fun. It's about free choice and true faithfulness. I know you clearly don't see it that way considering the path you've chosen, but Emma isn't like you, Willa. She's steadfast and faithful and knows exactly what she's doing."

Auntie Willa was taken aback, but her arm never left Emma's shoulders.

"Jodie, please. I took this decision just as seriously as you did. I just used me 'free choice' a different way is all. I'm sorry that meant things had to turn out the way they did, but it was my choice. Just like this will be Emma's. So if Emma wants to have fun, we're gonna have fun! And if she doesn't, well, what are the odds of that?"

She gave Emma a subtle wink and playful jab at her side, knocking her a little off balance. She regained her footing and spoke up the newly found courage that having her aunt's support provided.

"If it were up to me I wouldn't even be going. Mama, you asked me to do this, so I'm going to do it, but you can't ask me not to have fun. You have to trust me to do the right thing. I don't plan on doing anything in Chicago that I wouldn't do here."

Auntie Willa scoffed gently at this.

"Sweetie, I wouldn't say that. Even riding the elevator up to my apartment is going to be something you wouldn't do here, but I get what you're saying. You and your mother both can rest assured knowing that I would never make you do something you weren't up for. Cross my heart."

She made an "X" in the air over her chest with her right index finger, but Mama didn't look convinced with her arms crossed over her own chest.

"You have to trust me to do the right thing," Emma interjected through the tension.

"Sweetheart, of course I trust you." Mama walked over to her daughter and embraced her. "I know it doesn't seem like it at the moment, but I'm proud of you and grateful that you're doing this. God will guide you. As long as you follow your heart and His word you'll make it through."

She kissed Emma on the top of her head and reluctantly let her go.

"I love you Emma."

"I love you too, Mama. Don't worry about me. I'll make the most of it."

Emma then walked over to her sister and gave her a hug goodbye while she chattered away about clothes, boys, and Navy Pier. She tried to soak up as much of Abigail's excitement as she could before picking up her bag and walking out the door. Mama and Abigail followed them out to the car. When she saw the vehicle, Abigail let out an excited scream and ran over to it.

"It's red!" she yelled back at Mama and Emma, as if she thought they couldn't see it yet. Emma approached more cautiously. It seemed safe enough, by the looks of it, but she knew it could move ten times as fast as any buggy. She imagined the car being pulled along by two of her family's horses and allowed herself a small smile. Auntie Willa offered to help Emma with her bag just as she got close enough to run her fingers along the cool, smooth surface of the car. The trunk popped open on it's own and made Emma jump. Auntie Willa dangled the keys in front of Emma's surprised face.

"Cool, huh?" she said with a grin. Emma only smiled back and nodded. "Well, it's time to hit the road. If you forgot anything we can just pick it up when we get into the city. Bye, Abigail! Bye, Jodie! I'll try to get her back here in one piece!"

Auntie Willa opened the passenger side door for Emma and she slipped inside. She watched her aunt walk around the car to her own side and hop in, flashing Emma a faux-nervous smile. Emma watched her aunt pull the seatbelt around her body and clip it into the buckle.

She took the cue and, after a little bit of fumbling, was safely buckled in. Auntie Willa put the key in the ignition and the car started with a low roar.

"You ready, Em? No turning back now!"

Emma didn't know if she was ready, but she knew she had to be.

"Yes, Auntie Willa. Let's go."

"That's the spirit!" Auntie Willa replied joyously as she pressed a button next to her to open the front two windows. "Wave to your mom and sister. They're gonna miss you!"

Emma stuck her hand out the open window and looked back at her family standing outside. Abigail could barely contain herself as she fidgeted from foot to foot waving frantically. Mama was her opposite, standing tall and still, neither happy nor unhappy about seeing her oldest daughter drive away to Chicago. Emma pulled her hand back inside just as the car began to move. Her stomach lurched, but the feeling receded the farther they drove from home. Auntie Willa turned on the radio and started humming along. Emma kept her eyes locked on the road in front of them, watching her neighbor's homes fly by out of the corner of her eye. Auntie Willa's words echoed in her mind. *No turning back now!* She was tempted to turn around to see what her house looked like from this far away, but she took those words literally. There will be time to turn around later, she reminded herself, but this was the beginning of a new journey and she was determined to face it head on.

***

The view outside Emma's window slowly morphed from just ripened soy and cornfields to suburban neighborhoods filled with cookie cutter homes and chain grocery stores. She spent the first hour or so of the drive silently watching the world around her change and she felt herself changing, just a little bit, with it. From the safety of the car she was slowly immersed in this new world and allowed herself to become accustomed to it, but she didn't know what to expect when she stepped out.

Auntie Willa had been mostly silent up until now. She happily sang to herself and understood that Emma was the type to quietly take things in before wanting to talk about them, but Auntie Willa was not that type and after an hour of quiet she had about reached her breaking point.

"Are you getting excited? I remember sitting on the edge of my seat about to burst when I left home for the first time."

"I guess I'm...surprised? I thought it would be harder to leave than it was. I thought things would feel more alien, but after passing through all of these towns that look the same it's starting to feel familiar. Does that make sense?"

'Totally! I was blown away by the first Target I saw, but by the ninth or tenth it definitely lost its mystery. Don't you worry, though, Chicago is gonna knock your socks off. I've lived there for almost two decades now and it still takes my breath away when I'm driving toward that skyline. I'm definitely gonna take you to the planetarium. You won't get a better view of the city, or the universe, from anywhere else. I swear, it'll change your life."

She agreed to go on this trip to reassure herself and her family that she wanted her life to stay the same. She hadn't given any thought to how she might come home changed. This thought both scared and excited Emma. For the first time, she allowed herself to think of the experience not just as a trial, but also as an adventure.

"I think I'd like that. Back at home the sky is filled with millions of stars at night. After dinner Abigail and I sometimes go out into the yard and lie down to look up at them. I know that most of them already have names, but we'd lie there and come up with names of our own. I usually picked names of people from the Bible. It's comforting to think God's people are looking down on us, but Abigail always named the stars after boys she likes," Emma giggled at the memory and Auntie Willa followed suit.

"You won't see many stars in Chicago. The sky's mostly filled with planes and helicopters, but you'll be able to see all sorts of things at the planetarium. All the stars named after your sister's crushes and then some!"

Emma tried to imagine how they got all the stars to fit inside one building when the entire skyline of Chicago rose up out of the rode in front of her. She'd never seen it before but she knew it couldn't be anything else. Auntie Willa glanced over at Emma and saw her eyes grow wide.

"Awesome, isn't it? Just you wait."

This feeling was not what Emma expected. She wanted to know what it felt like to be amongst those buildings, and all the people who live in them. She wanted to know how it felt to be a part of something so massive and seemingly intangible. The buildings look small on the horizon, but Emma was still struck by their size. She was so caught up imagining how it would feel to sit on top of the tallest building in Chicago and see the landscape change backward from city, to suburb, to home that she almost forgot she'd planned to go back.

***

Auntie Willa had prepped her for the elevator, but she still gripped the railing with white knuckles when it began its assent. Auntie Willa lived on the nineteenth floor of a high-rise with two bedrooms and a sweeping view of Lake Michigan. One bedroom was Auntie Willa's and Charlie had unofficially occupied the other until the day before. He was a little put out when Auntie Willa dragged his bed and toys out into the living room, but immediately changed his tune when he met Emma. She didn't even have a chance to realize that she'd never been this high up before Charlie bombarded her with doggy kisses. Emma's family didn't own any official pets, just their horses and some chickens, but she immediately warmed up to him.

"Charlie likes you! I knew he would," cooed Auntie Willa.

"I like him, too! We've never had a dog," Emma replied, scratching Charlie behind the ears.

"Well you do now. Mi perro es tu perro!"

"What?"

"Oh that's just a little Spanish for you. It means 'my dog is your dog.' I can teach you a little while you're here if you'd like."

Emma didn't know that Auntie Willa could speak another language. She was impressed by how worldly her aunt was, but then remembered that focusing her attention on things like that is what drew Auntie Willa away from the church in the first place.

"Maybe, but I don't know what good Spanish would do me back home."

It was clear Auntie Willa didn't agree, but she refrained from pushing the matter.

"Why don't you get settled in your room? Maybe hang up some of the clothes you brought, take a shower, and I'll order up some Chinese food. You ever have Chinese food? Probably not, but you'll love it. I swear!"

"Okay," was all Emma could muster. She had only ever eaten what Mama or their neighbors had cooked for her. The idea of "ordering" food was as unfamiliar as "Chinese," but she was uncomfortable denying Auntie Willa's hospitality. She took her bag into the spare room and began to unpack before cautiously figuring out how to work the shower.

When she got out of the bathroom she found a warm looking pair of sweatpants and a baggy t-shirt waiting for her on her bed.

"I know you probably brought a nightgown with you," Auntie Willa yelled from the living room, "but trust me, there's nothing cozier than a hand-me-down pair of sweatpants that are too big for you."

Not one to protest, she pulled on the black pair of pants and the shirt that said "Chicago Marathon 2013" on the front and met Auntie Willa in the living room where a feast of little white boxes, black plastic containers, and a mountain of fortune cookies was waiting for her.

"I didn't know what you liked so I got a little bit of everything. Plus, I told them we were having a party so they'd give me extra fortune cookies. Dig in!" She handed Emma a plate, a pair of chopsticks, and a fork just in case.

Between surprisingly delicious bites of fried rice and sesame chicken, Emma asked her aunt about the t-shirt.

"Did you run a marathon, Auntie Willa?"

"Ha! I just bought ten pounds of Chinese food. What do you think? No, my ex-boyfriend gave me that shirt while we were dating."

Emma was suddenly uncomfortable about the idea of wearing a man's shirt, and Auntie Willa could see that.

"Don't worry, girly, he hasn't warn that shirt in years so it practically never belonged to him in the first place."

This reassured Emma enough that she continued to wear the shirt but now she had more questions.

"Auntie Willa, how many boyfriends have you had?"

"Well that depends. I've officially had three serious boyfriends, but I've casually dated quite a few more."

This took Emma aback. Mama met Papa at a Sunday evening sing and that was that. The girls at home almost always end up marrying the first boy who takes them home in his buggy. The idea that Auntie Willa had dated more than one man, had even worn their clothes, shocked her. She wondered how many other men's t-shirts she had in her closet, but she didn't dare ask.

"Wow," she replied, "I've never even held hands with a boy."

Auntie Willa chuckled kindly, "Well let's see what we can do about that, huh?"

This made Emma blush wildly and spoon too much rice into her mouth to keep from having to respond.

***

Auntie Willa wasted no time fulfilling her promise to take Emma to the planetarium. The very next day, after gently insisting that Emma borrow some more of her clothes and that she "leave the bonnet at home, girly!" they hopped in a cab and made their way to the museum.

The Adler Planetarium sat out on its own at the tip of a peninsula that jutted way out into Lake Michigan. Driving towards the impressive domed building gave Emma the same sensation as when she first saw the Chicago skyline. She couldn't wait to get inside to see where they kept all the stars, but after the cab dropped them off at the entrance Auntie Willa put her hand on Emma's shoulder to stop her from immediately sprinting up the stairs to the front doors.

"Hold up! Turn around first. Don't you want to see what I was talking about?"

Emma turned and saw the same skyline that awed her from a distance magnified and close enough to touch. That impressive massiveness that she felt fifty miles away was now right on top of her. The beautiful weight of the city was balanced on her small shoulders and she loved it. This feeling was enough to cause a small chip in Emma's resolve to return home, and this frightened her. She spun around on her heal, as if not being able to see the skyline made it not exist. She wasted no time climbing the stairs to the planetarium now. She relied on the familiarity of the stars to remind her of why she wanted to go home, but she didn't count on what else she would find inside.

***

After wandering around the exhibits for a while, taking in every fact about space, the stars, and especially the Sun that she could find, Auntie Willa suggested that they sit for a while and see a show. They decided on one called *Skywatch Live!* which showed how the night sky above Chicago would look if the city turned off all of its lights. This one interested Emma the most. She wanted to see how different the sky is here as opposed to at home.

Soon after they took their seats in the huge, domed theater the lights dimmed and the starry Chicago sky was projected above them. Emma had to stifle a gasp as every star she'd ever seen and more swirled above them. She was loath to admit it to herself, but it was almost more magical than the real night sky at home. Wrapped up in the tableau unfurling in front of her, she was caught off guard when a voice projected across the audience.

"Welcome, everybody! Thanks for coming out to see *Skywatch Live!* with me. My name's Nathan, and I'll be your night sky tour guide today."

Nathan had a pleasant voice, confident but not too rough. Emma thought he sounded like he had a sense of humor that he wasn't quite ready to share with the audience yet. Then she thought she shouldn't be thinking about this strange man's voice at all and tried her best to focus on the stars.

"Later on tonight, you'll probably be able to see Saturn even with all of the city lights. Do you want to hear a bad joke about Saturn?" A smattering of people in the audience cheered him on. "Okay, don't hate me for this. Why does Saturn have rings?"

"Why?" the audience, including Auntie Willa, happily asked.

"Because God liked it so he put a ring on it! Saturn is not a single lady."

He was met with a mixture of laughter and groans from the audience. Emma didn't really understand the joke but she found herself laughing anyways. There was something about the way Nathan said his joke was bad that made her feel like he actually thought the opposite. She could tell by his voice that he amused himself and she couldn't help but feel endeared by that.

"I told you it was terrible! Let's move on. I'm embarrassed," Nathan continued, but Emma knew he wasn't.

Emma tried as she might to focus on the show but Nathan's voice kept drawing her in. She wanted to know more things about him; what he looked like, if he liked Chinese food, did he want to hold her hand. Her cheeks flushed at that thought. He didn't even know she was in the same room as him, let alone if he'd be interested in *that*. More than that, she didn't even know who he was really, just the sound of his voice. Just as she began to talk herself out of these feelings for Nathan, he concluded the show and told everyone to come see him if they had any questions about the show. This chance to talk to him face-to-face squashed all of the doubts in her mind as she scrambled to think of a question.

"Auntie Willa, I've got a question for Nathan. Do you mind if we stop and ask?"

Auntie Willa had a hunch about Emma's true intentions.

"Sure thing. I actually have to use the ladies' so how about we meet by the sun when you're through?"

"Great, thanks!" Emma replied before speeding away full of nervous energy.

Emma tried to slow down to give herself time to think of the perfect question but before she knew it she was standing in front of a tall brunette man with a kind face and a nametag that said "Nathan."

"Hey!" he greeted her, "Did you enjoy the show? Gotta question for me?"

Emma nodded and asked the first thing that came into her mind, "Why was your joke funny?"

Nathan was not expecting this question, but he hid his surprise behind an understanding smile.

"The joke about Saturn? It was a reference to a Beyonce song where she talks about some guy who wouldn't marry her. So, I guess the joke's funny for that reason, but also can you imagine God marrying a planet?" This made him laugh, but only confused Emma.

"Who's Beyonce?"

"Who's Beyonce? What are you, an alien?" he replied incredulously, but not unkindly.

Emma picked up on his playfulness and said, "No, at least I don't think so. I grew up out in the country where there isn't much music except for in church. I guess that might as well be another planet compared to here."

It turned out more than just his own jokes could make Nathan laugh. He let out a whoop and wasn't shy about it or his feelings.

'I like you!" he said, "What's your name?"

"Emma," she replied, her signature blush swept across he face, but the traditional shyness that usually came along with it wasn't there. In fact, she had never felt more confident. Against all odds, and especially against her own rules for herself, she liked him too. She felt a small pang of worry about what consequences she might face for these feelings, but she pushed them away at least for this moment.

Nathan stuck his hand out in front of him and said, "Nice to meet you, Emma. You already know my name, but would you like to know more about me?"

"Absolutely," she said as she excitedly shook his hand. This was the first thing she felt confident of since she got here. It was only after giving Nathan Auntie Willa's phone number that she realized they had held hands, and in that moment she felt more alive than any day she had back home. Emma was in love and terrified.

***

Emma didn't have to wait long by the phone before Nathan called. She and Auntie Willa talked about him that night after they got home from the planetarium. She was excited for Emma, but warned her not to get her hopes to high about some guy she just met. Emma wanted to explain that he was more than that, but didn't know how to put it into words. She was having a hard time understanding these feelings herself. Luckily, Auntie Willa was a young girl in love once, too, and understood that sometimes these things need to run their course.

"Hey! Is this Emma from the planetarium?"

Emma had made sure that Auntie Willa gave her a complete lesson on how to use the phone well before she actually had to answer it.

"It is! Is this Nathan, also from the planetarium?"

"Sure is. Now let me get straight to the point, because I'm sure you've heard enough of my disembodied voice. I want to take you to dinner. Do you eat on your planet?"

Emma couldn't help but giggle girlishly.

"Yes, of course we eat!"

"Perfect. I'll come by your place around six. I'm thinking it's about time you tried classic Chicago deep dish pizza."

"We definitely don't have that where I'm from, but it sounds great!"

"See you then, then. Buh-bye Emma."

"Goodbye!"

Emma couldn't believe what she was about to do. In her wildest dreams back home she never thought she would be going on a date with a man in the city, let alone enjoy it. Auntie Willa was right. Chicago was changing her and it was starting to become difficult not to think it's for the better.

****

Nathan took Emma on a handful more dates over the next few weeks before they finally came back to the planetarium. In that time she had learned his favorite color (red), how many siblings he had (two), his favorite book (*A Brief History of Time*), and he learned all that and more about her (sky blue, one, The Bible). But she couldn't help but feel that he was keeping something from her. He was almost unnervingly forthright with her, to the point where she felt like she could ask him anything, but when she asked why he worked at the planetarium he grew solemn. This only lasted a moment before he coolly replied, "because I love teaching people about space!" but she could tell that wasn't the real answer. It made her uncomfortable that she knew there was something Nathan was actively keeping from her, but she was so happily in love that she didn't want to push him away by prying.

At the planetarium, Nathan had arranged a private, after hours tour for the two of them. This was the first time she had been alone with him and that made her nervous, but excited. Nathan had been nothing but a gentleman to her the entire time they were dating. He could tell she had some reservations about becoming physical with him, and he respected that. They often held hands in the park and always hugged goodbye when he dropped her off at home, but had yet to kiss. He knew about her religion and the fact that she was only here for a couple more weeks, but every time she anxiously brought up the fact that their relationship had an expiration date he just held her close and told her not to worry about anything but that exact moment. Each time he held her, Emma could never see the sad smile Nathan had on his face.

They made the same rounds through the exhibits as Emma and Auntie Willa did the first time she came here, but this time there was no one else around and Nathan told her secrets about different artifacts on display. She loved every second of it, but couldn't help wondering about the one secret that he wouldn't share with her.

Eventually they made their way to the same theater where they first met. A starry sky was projected above them and on the floor at the front of the theater Nathan had arranged a romantic picnic, complete with different cheese, candles, and a bottle of champagne. Emma was so overwhelmed at the sight of this gesture that she kissed him right there in the doorway. She hadn't planned to, but her nervousness slipped out of her body the moment Nathan's lips touched hers. They were as soft as down, but the pressure he put behind them made it seem like they might never part. Nathan softly grabbed the back of Emma's neck with one hand and held her waist with the other. She instinctively wrapped her arms around his neck and pulled his body as close to hers as she could without fusing them together.

This kiss was like seeing the city for the first time. It was like the first bite of Chinese food. It was lying on the grass looking at the stars. It was sunrise.

When they finally parted she could see that Nathan was silently crying.

"Nathan! What's wrong? Should I not have done that?"

"No!" he said chuckling through the tears, "You definitely should have done that." He sighed and touched her cheek. "I've got to tell you something. Will you sit down with me?"

Emma felt a knot in her stomach as Nathan lead her to the blanket surrounded by candles. He popped open the champagne, poured them both a glass, and said, "You're beautiful."

"Is that what you had to tell me?"

"It's one thing, but it's not *the* thing."

The way he said *"the* thing" made it sound like some sort of storybook monster.

"Just tell me. You're making me nervous."

"Emma... I'm dying. Like, really, incurably, probably quickly dying."

Emma couldn't say anything. At first, she thought this was just another of his bad jokes but it became clear by the tears welling in his eyes that he was serious. She threw herself into his lap and cried with him, spilling the champagne onto the blanket. They held each other quietly for a while before Emma finally spoke.

"I love you."

"I love you, too"

In that moment nothing else mattered to Emma. Her home, her family, God were all forgotten as she lay there on the floor with this surprising man that wasn't even supposed to be a part of her life. Now he felt like a permanent fixture. That night she decided she could ask for forgiveness later. They had found somehow each other in an infinite universe and that was a gift more precious and unique than any other. They made love in the theater that night under the stars.

***

Emma stayed in the city just long enough to go to Nathan's funeral. She wore a simple black dress that Auntie Willa lent her. The funeral was held in a Catholic church filled with ornamentation, extravagant robes, and subdued singing. She couldn't help but feel that Nathan would have wanted something simpler, more light hearted, but who was she to say? Her first love had come and gone like a comet. She broke her own rules, as well as God's and had nothing left to show for it. When the priest called everyone up to take communion, Emma just shook her head and cried. He understood, said a blessing over her, and sent her back to her seat. She didn't understand the tradition, but felt oddly comforted by it.

When she got back to Auntie Willa's she couldn't talk at all. Emma went straight to bed and shut the door. Tomorrow she was supposed to return home. She lay awake in bed for hours thinking about if that's what she really wanted after all. Around five in the morning she gave up trying to sleep and started to pack. She left the blinds open that night and soon her room was filled with pink and orange light. The sun rising over Lake Michigan painted the sky and made the water look like light. She watched the top of the sun peek over the horizon and slowly fill the sky. "This is a new beginning," she reminded herself, "Not just for me, but for Nathan, too."

The sight of something so familiar, but all together new gave Emma the answers she needed. Looking out over the painted lake, she knew she would be okay.

END

SMALL TOWN CHURCH ROMANCE

CHELSEA BECKS

"YOU WILL GO TO HELL. THE POWER OF CHRIST COMPELS YOU. THE POWER OF CHRIST WILL SAVE YOU IF YOU BELIEVE IN HIM. THE POWER OF CHRIST WILL KEEP YOU FROM HELL. GET YOUR ACT TOGETHER AND BELIEVE IN GOD."

Sara was a little freaked out.

Okay . . . Sara was really freaked out.

"So my cousin is a pharmacist and she can totally sneak me some Valium for this guy," Miranda, next to her, whispered in her ear.

Sara only went to church because it was routine. That wasn't to say she wasn't a pretty good Christian; she never killed anybody and she didn't eat meat on Fridays. Sometimes she prayed before she went to bed, and she never said the Lord's name in vain. Well. She tried not to.

"Look at that vein that bulges in his neck," Sara whispered to Miranda.

"Watch it burst," Miranda said smugly.

Sara tried not to smile.

No one in the congregation was okay with Pastor Henry being a total freak show. In fact it was completely surprising that their old pastor, Pastor Samuel, had picked him for his replacement at all. The young guy was new in town, and seemed to be totally normal, but how did he pass the job interview? Sara imagined Pastor Samuel in Boca or wherever he was, having a good laugh about his little practical joke, before informing all of them that the real Pastor would start next Sunday.

"He's kind of cute," Callie, from the other side of Miranda, said.

"Gross," Sara and Miranda said in unison.

Pastor Henry didn't hear any of this. "DO YOU THINK WHAT YOU ARE DOING IS OKAY? DO YOU REALIZE JESUS DIED FOR ALL OF YOU AND ALL YOU DO IS DISOBEY THE WORD OF GOD. REAL CLASSY. REALLY REALLY CLASSY. JUST YOU WAIT. JUST YOU WAIT FOR THE GLORIOUS DAYS OF REVELATION! YOU KNOW THE RIVER? THE TOWN RIVER? I WANT YOU ALL THERE TOMORROW AT SUNSET! THERE I WILL REPENT YOU OF YOUR SINS AND YOU WON'T ROT IN HELL LIKE YOU SHOULD!"

"Pop," Miranda whispered.

"TO QUOTE REVELATION:
BUT THE FEARFUL, AND UNBELIEVING, AND THE ABOMINABLE, AND MURDERERS, AND WHORE MONGERS, AND SORCERERS, AND IDOLATERS, AND ALL LIARS, SHALL HAVE THEIR PART IN THE LAKE WHICH BURNETH WITH FIRE AND BRIMSTONE: WHICH IS THE SECOND DEATH!
AVOID THE SECOND DEATH MY PARISHIONERS. AVOID THE SECOND DEATH AND FIND JESUS IN YOUR HEART. MEET ME AT

THE RIVER AT SUNSET. THE RIVER AT SUNSET. BE THERE OR ROT IN HELL!"

After church, everyone usually met in the hall for coffee hour. The girls did as not to say no to free food, but they noticed the crowd was a little thinner than usual.

"I wonder if he's gonna keep screaming?" Miranda asked, helping herself to a donut.

"It was kind of hot," Callie said.

"You're weird. You two deserve each other in hell."

The girls were then interrupted by the presence of Miss Hattie: the church clerk who was as wide as she was tall . . . and she was pretty tall. She plowed right between the group and helped herself to two donuts. "Hey, girls!" she said, the natural volume of her voice set to "loud". Her church dress that she wore every week was a dusty rose color with bright blue flowers and purple polka dots, her gray hair set in curls around her face.

"Hey, Miss Hattie," the three said in unison.

"Isn't it nice that even though your parents are dead all you girls still come to church?" She smiled brightly.

"Our parents aren't dead," Callie said, acknowledging herself and Sara.

"And my parents have been dead my whole life." Miranda had lived with her aunt and uncle since she was a baby.

"Oh." It was clear that Miss Hattie's memory was evading her, but she would never admit it. She smiled, and the girls noticed a streak of lipstick on her front teeth. "Well, anyway, we like to see young folk in the congregation."

"Is that why Pastor Samuel appointed a young minister?" Sara wondered. If anyone was going to spill the details on the parish's opinion of Pastor Henry it was going to be Miss Hattie.

Miss Hattie pursed her lips. "Well, now, you see I told Pastor Samuel that appointing a woman wouldn't be a bad idea. You know Rose Becker? Her daughter Lucy has just gotten her license or whatever they call it and she's a wonderful preacher, has a presence, and she's not too pretty so following the word of God might be able to find her someone. Anyway, I suggested to Pastor Samuel to appoint Lucy, and did he listen to me? Nope! He just appointed Henry, and I gotta say girls, he's a bit too aggressive for my liking."

The girls nodded in agreement, and Sara was grateful Callie didn't mention how cute she thought he was.

Before the conversation could progress, Pastor Henry was next to them. Close up, Sara noticed he wasn't a bad looking guy. He had dusty blonde hair, brown eyes, and nice features. He didn't look the least bit scary at all up close. He didn't even having the vein popping out of his neck.

"Hello," he said. Even his voice was quiet. "I'm just trying to go around and meet everyone."

"Well, you already met me," Miss Hattie said, clearly offended.

"Yes, Miss Hattie, I have met you." He even smiled, and Sara noticed it was a nice smile. "And you are all . . ?

"Calliope Calavant," Callie said. She completely made that up. Her real name was Callie Smith, but whenever she was meeting a new guy she liked to sound exotic.

"Miranda," Miranda said. "I don't have a last name."

Sara decided that since they were in a church she should be honest. "Sara Clevenger," she said. "Nice to meet you."

"Nice to meet all of you." Henry nodded. "I hope to see you all at the river tomorrow night. It really will be a fun time."

"Can you promise that?" Callie asked. The other two rolled their eyes.

"Yes," he laughed, but Sara noticed that Henry was looking at her when he said it. "I can promise that."

The girls went to brunch like they usually did on Sundays, and then Sara rushed home. Her mother had just left for work, picking up an extra shift at the bar she worked at, which meant her father was alone. He couldn't be that way for too long.

"Hey dad," Sarah said. Her father, Bill, was sitting in the recliner watching TV, his wheelchair next to him. He was dressed in his usual sweatpants and black T-shirt, his mouth open slightly as he looked at his daughter. He smiled. "Did you eat lunch yet?"

Bill managed a little nod. He couldn't speak. He had ALS, a diagnoses that tore Sara's family apart emotionally, but they still managed to stay together. Sara moved back home while her mother worked more to help take care of her dad.

"Are you comfy?" Sara asked, but then proceeded to fluff the pillow behind his back a little more. She looked at the TV. He was watching the baseball game, so at least he was actually entertained and not faking it for the amusement of his wife.

"Are you OK?" Sara asked.

Bill looked at her, and nodded. Sara couldn't help but smile at her father. "Okay," she said.

Henry lived in the rectory next to the church. He never had to pay rent and it was well lined so it was never too cold. He liked making a fire and drank tea every night while doing his Bible readings.

As he read that night, his mind flicked back to church. He knew his methods were extreme, but his favorite pastor had the same approach and where he grew up everyone loved the way that he preached. He wasn't sure how the new church felt about it, however. They all looked a little scared.

He then thought about Sara. The other two girls she was with were pretty, but there was something about her that really stood out to him. Maybe because she didn't have that pinched look on her face like Miranda, or because she didn't immediately try to jump in his pants like Callie. She was calm, and polite, and . . . beautiful.

He wasn't too sure about the meeting at the river the next day, but he was positive that she would show up. She did look interested when he mentioned it . . . unless he totally imagined that she did.

Henry looked out the window, wrapping his fingers around his warm tea cup and watched as the sun began to set. His street had the most perfect view of the horizon. He wondered if Sara liked sunsets.

Henry shook his head, and hoped that she would show up to the river. He hoped that she would like it. He hoped the whole town would.

That night, after Sara had put Bill to bed, her mother Nancy came home, finding Sara in the kitchen doing dishes. Nancy was a woman that aged too quickly. Having a dying spouse would do that to you. She was still pretty though, with blonde hair like her only daughter, and blue eyes. She worked hard at the bar, and made pretty good money. She needed to to take care of Bill.

"Hungry?" Sara asked. "I made Dad scrambled eggs. I could whip you up some."

Nancy collapsed at the table and shook her head. "I ate at work. How did he do?"

Sara bit her lip. "He didn't eat much. He tried to, but I don't think he was that hungry."

Nancy nodded, not bothering to hide how unbelievable exhausted she was. "How was church? The new preacher started today, didn't he?

"He wants to dunk us all in the river to repent us of our sins," Sara said, dropping the plate she was holding as the water suddenly got really hot. She turned down the dial and braved to pick it up again. "He's pretty crazy. He screamed the entire time instead of just giving a normal sermon. It was really uncomfortable."

"He probably just doesn't understand the way we are used to things." Nancy always tried to sympathize with things that were generally not well liked. Her favorite animal was the opossum.

"Or he's crazy," Sara laughed.

"I want you to go to that river dunk thing tomorrow," Nancy said. "Just give it a try. It's important we support members of the community. That church has helped us out so much since your father got sick, it's the least you could do."

Sara didn't want to argue with her mother. She didn't want to go, but she knew that if it was important to Nancy than it should be important to her. She decided not to ask Miranda and Callie if they were going too. She didn't want to get laughed at.

At seven o'clock the next evening, Henry waited by the river. It was the main water source in town, leading right into the reservoir. He figured the river would be a good place for the re-baptism of the congregation. He loved water. He loved its healing spirit. He hoped everyone else would too .No one was there yet, but he realized that "sunset" was a bit of a vague time. Maybe everyone else did not read the same solar clock he did and would be there in a little bit. He checked his watch. 7:01.

At quarter after, he checked his watch for the umpteenth time. No one was there yet. Henry could feel his smile begin to fade.

7:30, the sun was beginning to be a peachy color, and night was beginning to overtake the sky when he heard the car pull up. It parked on the grass, and the driver got out. It took him a second to realize it was Sara, and suddenly it did not matter that no one else in the congregation had showed up to the baptism.

"Pastor Henry," she said.

"It's just Henry."

She nodded. "Henry."

"Sara."

"Are you going to scream at me while you dunk me in the river, or is it completely okay if I just go about and do this myself?"

He felt a little uneasy. "I can give you a blessing," he said. "And I promise I won't scream."

She took off her shirt, and while the motion caught him off guard, Henry realized that she was wearing a one piece bathing suit. She stripped off her jean, and stood on the grass, curling it under her toes. He then took off his pants to his swim suit, and hesitated about his shirt, before realizing that it really didn't matter, then took it off. He was happy that for the first time in his life he was actually in somewhat good of shape, then realized how wrong it was of him to be thinking like that when he was about to baptize someone.

Him and Sara walked toward the river. He dunked his foot in, and realized the water was just a little bit warmer than ice. This would be quick. Sara, meanwhile, did not hesitate. She plunged right in, under the water, the light current not swaying her a bit. She resurfaced, and slicked her wet hair off her face with her hands before smiling. "Was that too premature for a blessing?" she asked.

"No," Henry replied, awing at how beautiful she looked in the sunset.

"It's better just to go right in," she explained. "Otherwise you'll be shivering. This way your body gets used to it."

Henry supposed she was right. He hadn't swam since summer camp when he was a kid; and even then he barely ever did. He was too busy reading a book to socialize with the other kids. Henry had never been much of a people person, even as a child. He turned to the church and his faith and the pastor who taught him so much, and only then was he able to find any comfort in himself.

Henry decided to just go for it, and dove right into the icy water, feeling it seep through his skin and freeze his veins. When he came up for air, he gasped, and then registered that Sara was laughing at him. He stood up, and shook his hair, before saying, "How the hell did you do that?"

"Did you just say hell?" she mused.

"I'm human, you know," he muttered.

Sara grinned. "Okay, so this baptism or whatever . . . let's just do this."

Henry nodded, then waded through the water so that he was standing right next to Sara. "I do this for you. I do this for your soul."

She nodded, and maybe he was imagining it, but she seemed to be staring at him.

"I'm going to dip your head in the water now."

She was treading in the shallow water, and he held her forehead as she dipped her hair under the water. He tried not to run his fingers through her hair. He tried to be professional, as he recited:

Living and Loving Father,

I praise and thank You with my heart for the liberation You have given me from the clutches of sin and Satan. By Your death on the Cross of Calvary, You have put my old life with its sin and judgment to death forever, and endowed me with a new life that is abounding with joy.

Father, I commit this Baptism Day into Your most precious and loving hands. I believe that by Your crucifixion on the Cross, my old self was rendered powerless and I was freed from all sin. You were raised from the dead that I too may live a life victorious and overcoming all evil.

Father, this day, I rededicate myself to live in You and live a life for Your glory. I remember the day when I was baptized and washed off all my sins. Lord, it is Your grace that I must be counted worthy to be called Your child. Help me to keep Your commandments. Renew my strength this day that I may be strong in faith and increase in zeal. Preserve me for the glorious day of Your coming. I believe Your Word which says, "He who has begun a good work in you will complete it until the day of Jesus Christ." Let this day be the beginning. Lead me into greater spiritual depths even in the coming days. In Jesus' precious name I pray.

Amen.

Henry traced the cross on her forehead with his thumb. "Amen," he whispered again, and then gently helped Sara lift her head up.

They locked eyes for a second, and that was when Henry noticed his hand was around her waist. Sara noticed too, but she did not try to stop it, in fact she felt like it should be there.

"So I'm not going to hell?" she whispered.

"No way," he whispered back.

Before he could acknowledge that it was happening, he was kissing her, or was she kissing him? They were kissing each other, and behind them the sun officially set.

The darkness over came the river, and noticing that their visibility was waning, Sara and Henry stopped before getting out of the river. Henry did not know what to say to her, other than a slew of apologies that was normal for him to spurt out in this type of situation. However, instead, he noticed she was smiling and said, "Was that okay?"

Sara laughed. "That was fine."

She realized she didn't bring a towel, so she put her clothes on over her soaking wet bathing suit. Henry put on his shirt, and then felt a little awkward about the situation. Even though kissing Sara was better than he imagined, he realized then he really did not know her at all, and to her he was just the screaming preacher.

"I'm sorry." His familiar words came out of his mouth.

"I kissed you," she said, giving him a weird look.

"I thought I kissed you?"

They were quiet for a second, and then both laughed.

Sara didn't expect any of that to happen, except for maybe the fact that she would be the only one to show up for the baptism ritual by the river. Flushed, and feeling happy for whatever reason, she went home to shower, and then proceeded to get ready for a night out with Callie and Miranda.

They all met at their favorite restaurant outside of town, where on Mondays the cocktails were half price after nine. Miranda wore a low cut sweater, and Callie an even tighter one. Sara tried not to smile to broadly when she sat down at the table.

"Who did you lay?" Callie asked.

"No one," Sara muttered, taking a sip of the martini her friends had already ordered her. She knew how the others felt about Henry, and since she didn't know if she really liked him yet she figured she should maybe keep the events of the evening to herself.

"Boring." Miranda rolled her eyes.

They all ordered a variety of appetizers, and the conversation as usual took a turn to talking about hot men. A little tipsy, Sara tried her best to keep her mouth shut, but eventually she was dying with curiosity.

"Henry is pretty hot," she said.

"Pastor Henry?" Callie asked. "Hell yeah."

"Nope." Miranda winced and shook her head. "Absolutely not. Nuh uh. No way."

"I think I like him," Sara said, and then she slurped her martini instead of looking at her friends for their reactions. When she deemed enough time had passed, she dared a glance, and saw both of them with their mouths wide open, not unlike a fish above water.

"Don't do it!" Miranda warned.

"Don't!"

"Think of your father!"

"Think of the women and children!"

"He's CRAZY!"

"ABSOLUTELY insane!"

"Even Miss Hattie didn't like him!"

It was clear that Miranda and Callie were getting hysterical. Around them, other people in the restaurant began to stare, and Sara was getting more and more uncomfortable. She was not expecting this much of an outburst.

"Okay, okay!" Sara held her hand up to silence them. "Keep your pants on. I won't do anything about it."

Although her friends looked relieved, deep inside Sara felt a little hurt. She tried not to imagine kissing Henry for the rest of the reason, but she found it really hard not to.

Henry was sitting in his office the next day writing a sermon when he heard the knock on the door. "Come in," he said.

The door opened, and he didn't bother to look up, figuring it was just Miss Hattie, when a familiar and beautiful voice said, "We need to talk."

He looked up and saw Sara there. She was wearing a dress, her hair tied back, and even though she wasn't dripping wet in the sunset she was still beautiful. Henry thought she may be too good to be true. "Sara," he said. "Come in."

She did, which he took as a good sign. He was glad he cleaned off his desk that morning; he didn't want her thinking he was a slob. Sara sighed. "We have to talk . . . about your preaching."

"You don't like it?" he asked.

"You're a little . . . aggressive," Sara said, and then she bit her lip. "It's scaring all of your friends."

"You're scared of what your friends think?" Maybe Sara was one of those shallow girls that Henry had known growing up. He couldn't help but feel a pit of disappointment form in his stomach.

"My friends . . . the town . . ." Sara winced. "You're just so different from Pastor Samuel. He was gentle and sweet and at first I thought that maybe the aggressive and angry, brimstone and fire speech was just what you were, but after what happened at the river . . . you're a nice guy, Henry. You're kind and charming and the person who baptized me and the person who was screaming Revelation were not the same person."

"Pastor Samuel knew what he was hiring," Henry said, feeling a little angry. "He knew what my style was and he liked it and when I was hired . . . he knew what he was getting."

"We don't know if it was a joke though."

Sara regretted it the moment she said it. Henry, meanwhile, did not know her well enough to figure that out. He stood up and pointed to the door. "I think you should leave."

"Henry . . ."

"Now."

She stood up and made her way to the door. Before she left though, she turned around and said, "I really liked the kissing, by the way. I really like you."

And with that, she left, and Henry was more confused and hurt than ever.

Sara cried in the car on the way home, to get it out of her system before she saw her father and she had to be strong for him. She wiped her face, and reapplied her mascara, before going inside the house. Her father was sleeping in his wheelchair in the kitchen; the warmest room in the house because of the sunlight that swallowed the room through the big bay window.

She decided not to disturb him, and made herself a peanut butter and jelly sandwich. As she ate, she watched her father. His chest was rising and falling slowly; he was still breathing. She knew she only had months more with him, and dreaded the moment when his chest would no longer rise and fall and he would be nothing more than a memory. His disease was always fatal, and there was nothing she could do about it but enjoy the time she had left with him.

When she was done eating, Bill opened his eyes.

"Hey, Dad," she said.

He tried to smile.

"I think I might have done something stupid.

When her father was functional, the two were close. Now, however, since he could not spill all of her secrets to the world, Sara found herself telling him everything that was on her mind. Since he could smile and sometimes shake his head, it was a sort of effective way of communication. It made her feel better at least.

"I kissed the pastor."

Bill opened his eyes wider.

"Not Pastor Samuel. Pastor Henry. The new pastor. He's young, and kind, and super socially awkward . . . he's a really great guy. I can tell. But he's a yeller. He screams about Satan and he wanted to dunk everyone in the river to repent their sins and . . . no one likes him. No one. Not Miranda or Callie or Miss Hattie . . ."

Bill didn't say anything, or even react.

"I don't know what to do, Dad."

Suddenly, Sara thought her father was choking. He started making noise, and she ran over to him, but Bill tried to push her aside as best as he could. She stopped, and looked at her father, and his eyes widened a little more. "Give," he stammered. "Him. A Ch-ch-chance."

Sara teared up: her father hadn't spoken in over a month. "Dad?"

He coughed a little, and then swallowed, and nodded., then smiled.

"Give him a chance?"

Bill nodded.

If it had been any other person besides her father, who had used all of her strength to tell her that, she most likely would have ignored it. "Okay," Sara nodded, still teared up. "I will."

Henry thought a lot about what Sara had told him, and as much as he did not want to listen to a woman and do what she told him to do, he also had to take in account what was best for his congregation.

He arranged a meeting with Miss Hattie and, just like Sara had told him, she agreed that his sermons needed to die down a little bit. Henry called up Pastor Samuel, who said that hiring Henry was not a joke, but he hoped that he would learn his lesson and arrange his sermons to be friendlier. He also wished Henry luck with Sara, and hoped the best for him.

Henry spent the last few days of the week to write Sunday's sermon. He hoped Sara and the rest of the congregation would like it.

On Sunday, he dressed in his robes, and began the service. He spoke quietly, but not too quiet, and tried not to let his nerves get the best of him. He tried not to look at Sara too much, but there she was: sitting in the second row with her wretched friends, a small smile on her face the entire time.

Then, it was time for the sermon. Again, he spoke quietly, and firmly, and then when it was close to an end, he said, "I am new in town. I am a new preacher, and you are a new community. As many of you know Jesus was a stranger in many lands amongst his travels, and although his methods weren't as . . . extreme . . . as mine, he did get some ridicule. But there were also those that gave him a chance, and those who helped him become well known and lead him down the road for him to help him save us. I want us all to grow as a community and to become followers of Jesus and God together, so today, I propose that after service we all go down to the river and pray together, and wash away all of our sins and start a fresh. A new community. A new start. And now, I want to pray:

Great Redeemer and Father of all nations, I humbly come before your throne and offer my thanks and praise for all that you have done to bless us, your people. Please let me know you and be aware of your daily presence in my life. Forgive me, dear Father, when I haven't been a suitable place for your grace and name to dwell. Thank you for redeeming me from the sin that once entangled me. Guard my heart and rescue me from the deceptive lies of the evil one. In Jesus' name, and I say his prayer, Our father, who art in heaven, hallow by thy name, thy kingdom come, thy will be done, on earth as it in in heaven. Give us this day our daily bread, and forgive our trespasses, as we forgive those who trespass against us, and lead us not into temptation, but deliver us from evil, for thine is the kingdom and the power and the glory forever. Amen.

"Amen," the congregation echoed after him. When Henry lifted his head from prayer, he saw Sara smile at him.

After church, Henry skipped the coffee hour, and went right to the river. He did not expect anyone to come, but he figured maybe it would be okay. He had prayer and, he hoped, he had Sara.

She showed up first, a couple minutes after he did. She brought a blanket. They laid it on the grass and sat next to each other, finding calm in watching the river gently roll by. They didn't talk for a moment, but then Henry realized she was holding his hand.

"A week ago, I never would have expected this," Sara finally said.

"Me either."

"A week ago, I never thought that I would be falling in love with you."

Henry looked at her, and the two of them locked eyes. She smiled, and he felt like he could kiss her, but then the sound of a car came, pulling up. He didn't know the names of the people coming towards them, but he knew they were members of the church. He stood up, breaking away from Sara, to greet them. When he extended his hand they took it, and that was a good sign.

Soon, more and more people showed up. Some brought food. One brought a portable grill. It wasn't the type of baptism Henry was expecting, but he found himself helping the guy set it up and helped make burgers for everyone. A few kids brought frisbies. Some people swam in the river. Miranda and Callie even showed up and, although Miranda's stare was still uncomfortable, Henry took it as a good sign that she was there.

Eventually, after everyone had eaten, Henry took them all into the river. He instructed everyone to get into pairs, and they would do this twice, each time one person holding their partner up as he read them the prayer of baptism and helped them wash away all of their sins. The entire congregation of roughly 100 people paired up and waded into the river, and he blessed them with the same prayer he blessed Sara:

Living and Loving Father,
I praise and thank You with my heart for the liberation You have given me from the clutches of sin and Satan. By Your death on the Cross of Calvary, You have put my old life with its sin and judgment to death forever, and endowed me with a new life that is abounding with joy.
Father, I commit this Baptism Day into Your most precious and loving hands. I believe that by Your crucifixion on the Cross, my old self was rendered powerless and I was freed from all sin. You were raised from the dead that I too may live a life victorious and overcoming all evil.
Father, this day, I rededicate myself to live in You and live a life for Your glory. I remember the day when I was baptized and washed off all my sins. Lord, it is Your grace that I must be counted worthy to be called Your child. Help me to keep Your commandments. Renew my strength this day that I may be strong in faith and increase in zeal. Preserve me for the glorious day of Your coming. I believe Your Word which says,

"He who has begun a good work in you will complete it until the day of Jesus Christ." Let this day be the beginning. Lead me into greater spiritual depths even in the coming days. In Jesus' precious name I pray.
Amen.

At the end, most of the people continued swimming when Sara noticed another car pulling up, squeezing in between two other cars that had unevenly parked on the grass. She thought . . . but it couldn't be.

Nancy was pushing Bill toward the river before she knew it, and Sara couldn't help but smile. Her father had not left his house in a long time, and it was truly a miracle that he was strong enough to be able to at all.

"Henry," Sara said to him. "I want you to meet my father."

The two walked toward Bill. Sara introduced Henry to her parents, and Bill smiled at the pastor. "You have a beautiful daughter," Henry told him.

Bill smiled wider.

"And honestly . . ." Henry blushed a little. "I think I'm falling in love with her."

Bill struggled, but a moment later, he was able to lift his hand enough for Henry to grab it. The two men shook hands, and around then a congregation celebrated becoming even closer together.

LOVINA'S HEART
DEIDRA SCOTT

Chapter One

Lovina Miller took a deep breath as she reached up to pull a piece of laundry from the clothesline and put it in the basket at her feet. Above her head, a pair of bluebirds danced through the bright June sky, reminding her that summer was quickly approaching.

Summer. It was a time full of fresh starts and new beginnings.

Looking across the yard, Lovina watched David Yoder working with one of her brothers. Together, the two young men were struggling with their task, trying to break her *daed's* new horse.

Ach, just watching David sent a thrill of excitement through Lovina's heart. Although she had known him most of her life, there was something about him that could still put a spark inside of her, giving her the feeling that they had just met.

Growing up, Lovina had always dreamed of marrying David. It had just seemed natural to her. With their two houses located side-by-side, they had spent all of their childhood hours playing together in the creek that wound between their properties and climbing the big apple tree like little monkeys.

Lovina had decided early on that she and David would grow old together, spending their adult days raising babies and making a life within their Amish community.

Now that Lovina had turned eighteen-years-old, she felt like she was stuck in the midst of a waiting game, simply counting down the hours until David came forward to begin their relationship together.

Smiling to herself, Lovina basked in the realization that, as an adult, it was now time to watch her childhood dreams start to unfold.

"*Danki* for the help, David!" Lovina heard her father call out from the barn and looked up in time to see David waving goodbye to her family as he started across the yard.

Lovina felt her heart go aflutter when, rather than take the path back to his own parents' house, David veered closer to her own home and made a bee-line right for the clothesline where she was working.

"*Gut* afternoon, David!" Lovina called out, her voice seeming somewhat weak to her own ears.

Watching him come closer, Lovina couldn't help but marvel at how handsome her childhood friend had become. With a head-full of dark red hair and sparkling blue eyes, David had always looked like a cheerful storybook character; however, as he aged, he grew tall and muscular, his boyish looks transforming into that of a good-looking man.

"Hello there, Lovina," David called back, rolling down his sleeves as he walked along, "I tell you, that horse of your *daed's* nearly got me down this time!"

Lovina smiled as she pulled a pair of her brother's pants off of the laundry line and tossed them in the basket, "I guess we should consider ourselves glad to have such a good horse-breaker living so near-by."

To her surprise, David's face suddenly seemed to darken. Taking a deep breath, he reached up and put one hand on the clothesline, "Actually, Lovina, I wanted to talk to you about that."

Although Lovina had hoped that David would want to talk to her alone, she could already tell that his news wasn't going to be what she had wanted to hear.

"Lovina," David looked out across the fields, "Ever since you had your birthday, I'd been hoping..." his voice trailed off and he gave a shrug, "Well, nothing I'd hoped for is going to work out this summer." Standing up taller, he announced, "My uncle from Indiana wrote telling about the need for a good horse-trainer in his community. I agreed to go help for the next three months...I'll be home in time to help my dad get started on the harvest."

Lovina felt her heart drop in her chest. The idea that David would leave had never entered her mind. Even though it was only for three months, it felt like it might as well be three years.

"*Ach*, Lovina, don't be so sad," David reached out and placed his hand on her arm, "I'll be back – I promise. Kentucky is my home...I sure don't have any plans to run off for good."

Something about having his hand on her arm made the pain a little more bearable. Looking up, Lovina met David's tender gaze with her own.

"When I come back..." David took a deep breath and kicked at a clump of grass with his foot. It was strange to see him so uncomfortable – David was usually one to be bold and daring, willing to say whatever was necessary.

"When I come back, I hope we can spend more time together," David managed to say, "Seems like we've grown apart over the years, and I'm ready for that to end."

Lovina couldn't stop the smile that spread across her face, "And maybe not be climbing trees this time?" She added.

David laughed, "Of course we'll be climbing trees again!" He teased.

Growing more sober, he lifted his hand and ran it gently across her cheek, "I'll see you in three months, 'Vina."

Three months. As she watched him walk away and back to his parents' farm across the creek, Lovina took a deep breath and tried to still her thumping heart. Three months was a long time – she was just glad that she had those tender moments to cling to during the summer that stretched out before her.

Chapter Two

Taking a deep breath, David watched out the passenger window as the driver he had hired took him farther and farther from his home in Kentucky and on toward his Uncle Amos' house in Indiana.

"Are you nervous about leaving home for so long?" David's paid driver, Mr. Simpson asked, as he flipped his turn signal on and proceeded toward Uncle Amos' house.

David shook his head and laughed, "*Ach*, no, not nervous."

"Anxious to get away from your parents?" Mr. Simpson asked with a chuckle.

"No, nothing like that." David assured him, "Just glad to be helping my uncle and the people in his community."

Leaning his head back against the headrest of the seat, David closed his eyes and thought about Mr. Simpson's question.

Was he glad to be getting away from his parents? Although he had been quick to assure his driver that wasn't he case, David wasn't so certain himself. To be completely honest, David wasn't a bit sorry to be leaving for the summer. While he had always loved his home and his family, David relished the chance to get away.

Since David had been a little boy, he had always known what was expected of him. He was going to settle down, buy a piece of property close to his parents, and marry Lovina Miller. It wasn't a bad plan at all, but it seemed so boring and dull. Deep in his heart, David had always dreamed of excitement and adventure. Maybe his trip to Indiana would finally provide him with a chance to enjoy his freedom before he settled down for good.

David's driver took him straight to Uncle Amos' house, helped him unload his bags, and then left him to head back to Kentucky.

Uncle Amos and his entire family were happy to welcome David to their home. Uncle Amos explained that everyone in the community could use his horse breaking services and that they would be bringing their horses to his house so that David could train them. Uncle Amos also said that, during David's spare time he could help the family out in the dry goods store they had located in a small shed next to the road.

"I'll take you out to the store now, so that I can show you what kind of work you can do out there." Uncle Amos suggested once David had put his clothes away in the spare bedroom.

Leading David across the yard, Uncle Amos explained, "Of course, I will pay you for helping in the store...and you can also have all the money for training the horses."

David shook his head, "*Ach,* that's too much, Uncle Amos. I'm happy to have the chance to help out."

Uncle Amos chuckled and reached out to give David a slap on the back, "Now, now, don't go talking like that. I'm sure a handsome young man like you should be saving back to buy a nice farm and making plans for the future. I'd dare say that some pretty girl back home has caught your eye."

David gave a shrug, not too anxious to think about his future, "Nothing set in stone just yet."

The graveled lane ended and the two men found themselves standing side-by-side outside of the dry goods store. Reaching out, Uncle Amos pushed the door open, revealing a building with shelves full of baking supplies, canned goods, and some craft items.

"Hannah!" Uncle Amos called out, as he led David through the small building, "Hannah!"

"I'm over here," a soft voice returned.

Turning the corner around one of the shelves, they found a young Amish woman on her knees, busy stacking bags of flour.

"Hannah, I want you to meet my nephew, David," Uncle Amos announced, "David, this is Hannah – she is my wife's cousin and she's helping us out in the store this summer."

Hannah pulled herself to her feet and turned to stare up at David with large, blue eyes. Wisps of dark hair had escaped her prayer *kapp*, making a sort of halo around her face.

Just looking at her, David felt his heart give a leap. She was so unexpectedly beautiful in a dark, mysterious way.

"*Gut* to meet you, David," Hannah replied timidly.

"David is likely to be helping out in the store when he isn't working with the horses," Uncle Amos explained. Giving David a pat on the arm, he motioned toward the back room, "Come on, I want to show you where I store the bulk supplies."

As David followed his uncle, he had a hard time even listening to what was being said. His mind was still mesmerized by the beautiful and timid young lady he had just met. David could hardly wait to get to know and learn more about Hannah.

Lovina sat on the edge of her bed, looking out across the fields of farmland through her bedroom window. Knowing that David was no longer in the house next-door left a hollow emptiness in Lovina's heart. In her eighteen-years, she had never gone a summer without seeing David.

Lovina tired to imagine what her sweet friend was doing at that moment. Did he realize how much she was thinking of him? Did he miss her at all?

Lovina closed her eyes and took a deep breath, "Dear God," she whispered into the darkness, "Please, bring the man that I love back to me."

Chapter Three

David carefully guided his uncle's buggy down the road. It was only his second day in Indiana and work was already starting to pick up; however, Uncle Amos had sent him to town to pick up some nails for a woodworking project he was doing in the barn.

The summer afternoon sun shone down on David and the warmth of the breeze put a smile on his face. David was enjoying his time away from home and, although he had not had many opportunities to spend time with Hannah, he had hopes that would change eventually.

The buggy suddenly took a lung, pulling David out of his thoughts.

"Woah, boy! Woah!" David pulled tightly on the reigns, unsure of what was happening to the buggy. Carefully guiding the horse to the side of the road, he jumped down from his seat and looked over the situation.

Something was wrong with the front buggy wheel. Grabbing a hold of it, David gave it a wiggle, trying to determine if it could keep going.

Pulling off his straw hat, David slapped it against his leg in frustration. He couldn't get to town on that wheel and he didn't think he could make it back to his uncle's house either.

The clipping of oncoming horse hooves made David stand up straighter and wave desperately at the approaching buggy.

The driver was a single Amish man. As soon as David caught his attention, the other driver pulled his buggy to the side of the road behind David.

"Hi there!" David greeted with a smile as he watched the other Amish man get off his buggy and start toward him, "Boy, I sure am glad to see you!" Sticking out a hand, he announced, "I'm David Yoder. I'm staying with my Uncle Amos Yoder – you probably know him."

The stranger nodded and simply said, "I'm Luke Christner." Taking a deep breath, he walked over to the buggy and squatted down to inspect the wheel.

"Looks like this is busted good," he announced, pushing his hat back on his head and reaching up to wipe some sweat from his brow.

David groaned, "I was afraid of that."

Standing to his feet, Luke continued, "I'm afraid you shouldn't drive it any farther than just a few feet or you'll end up wrecking or destroying your entire buggy." With a slight smirk, Luke added, "Lucky for you, this is my parents' drive right up ahead. And I just happen to work on buggies for a living."

David's eyes got large and he let out a huge sigh, "Oh, *gut*! Do you think that you could help me out?"

Luke nodded, "Sure thing. Just lead your buggy down to my workshop. I'll have her fixed up in just a bit."

True to his word, Luke had the buggy wheel fixed within an hour.

David stayed by the young man who had rescued him and worked to fill him in on all the details about his life, his home, and his family. Luke, who seemed to be more reserved, was happy to listen and donate very few details of his own.

"How much do I owe you?" David asked as Luke put the repaired wheel back on his buggy.

Luke gave a shrug as he secured the wheel in place, "Nothing. Consider it a welcome present. Maybe you can help me with one of my horses one day this summer."

"*Ach*," David raised an eyebrow, "I can't let you do that. I took some time you could have been working on other projects..."

Before he could finished, Luke started shaking his head, "No, no you didn't," he assured David as he stood up straight, "Honestly, I didn't have any other work for today." Sighing deeply, he announced, "As badly as we need a horse trainer in this area, we do not need any kind of buggy work. Jobs around here are scarce, David. I was glad to help."

David pondered Luke's statement for a moment. As an idea entered his mind, a broad smile spread across his face, "Listen, Luke! You may not be needed here, but you sure would be in my community! How would you feel about going to Kentucky to spend the summer with my family? It would sure help them out while I'm gone, and you could earn money doing buggy repairs and carpentry work!"

Luke was silent, obviously studying David's suggestion. Finally, with a shrug, he announced, "*Jah* – I don't see why that wouldn't be great. *Danki*, David."

The entire plan made David's face light up like that of a little boy. Grinning from ear-to-ear, he grabbed his new friend's hand in a shake and started making plans to get Luke back to Kentucky.

Chapter Four

Lovina reached up to wipe some sweat from her forehead as she took a break from chopping weeds out of the row of green beans. Despite all her hard work, the weeds were quickly starting to overtake the plants.

David had now been gone two weeks, and Lovina had yet to hear anything from him. His absence made her sad and she wished for all she was worth that she would receive a letter.

Glancing across the field toward his house, she thought of all the times they had snuck away from their chores and played together instead.

To her surprise, Lovina saw a young man approaching her. Could it be...? Lovina's heart dropped as he drew closer. Although she had hoped that it was David, she instantly realized that her eyes had been playing tricks on her. This stranger was even taller than her dear childhood friend and slightly thinner.

"Hullo," Lovina called out as he continued to draw closer.

"Hullo," the stranger returned, his voice deep and almost mysterious, "Are you Lovina Miller?"

Lovina stood up straighter and adjusted her prayer *kapp*, "That would be me. Do I know you?"

The stranger shook his head, "No, you don't." Now he was so close that Lovina was able to get a good look at him. This strange Amish man looked to be in his early twenties, but he seemed more mature. His brown hair was so dark it was almost black, and his eyes a dark color chocolate. Just looking at him made Lovina take a deep breath of surprise. *Ach*, it was hard to remember a time that she had ever seen such a *gut*-looking man!

"I'm Luke Christner. I know your friend, David, and I'm staying with his family until he returns." Glancing toward her house, Luke asked, "Is your *daed* at home? The Yoders told me that he has a construction crew and I'd like a job."

Lovina felt so out of sorts, she wasn't sure what to do. Looking down at her bare feet, she tried to gather her composure. Taking a deep breath, she said, "*Nee*, my *daed* isn't home from work yet, but we're expecting him any minute. If you'd like to wait in the house, my *mamm* can give you some fresh lemonade and cookies."

Luke glanced from the house back to Lovina and then shrugged, "If you don't mind, I'll just stay out here. Looks like you could use some help." Grabbing for an extra hoe, Luke set to work, removing the pesky weeds from among the rows of bean plants.

There was something about Luke that made Lovina feel uncertain about everything. He was a good help in the garden, but she certainly would have felt more at-ease without him. On the other hand, she dreaded him leaving once her father got home from work. Just being near him made her feel things that she had never experienced – she found herself overwhelmed by a sort of giddiness that sprung up from deep within. Although Lovina had always been a talker, she suddenly seemed almost speechless.

"You don't have to do this," Lovina assured him.

Luke simply set his jaw and turned to look at her with his brooding, dark eyes, "I don't have to...but I want to."

Lovina felt weak in the knees, as if she might keel right over. Taking a deep breath, she tried to stead herself.

Suddenly, she found herself a little glad that David was going to be gone for the summer. As quickly as the thought flitted through her mind, she pushed it away; however, just the realization that she could think such a thing left Lovina questioning everything about the future.

David washed his hands in a pail of water that had been set out by the barn, preparing himself for the evening meal. Inside the house, Aunt Miriam was putting the finishing touches on a pot of homemade chili with the help of three of David's cousins.

True to Uncle Amos' word, in the time that David had spent in Indiana he had already been so busy, he hardly had time to even think about being at home.

Wiping his clean hands on a towel, David glanced across the acres of land that his uncle owned. There, in the glowing darkness of the evening, he could make out the form of a young woman walking near the pond.

Hannah.

David had learned to recognize her from a distance. Even though it would be hard to distinguish her from any other Amish woman from so far away, David could pick Hannah out because she was always alone. It seemed like she carried an air of sadness with her, wherever she went.

Taking a deep breath, David stepped out of the barn and started the short walk to the pond.

"Hi there," David called out as he drew near to Hannah.

The young woman looked up at him and gave a sad smile.

"What are you doing?"

Hannah gave a shrug and pulled her black shawl tighter against her shoulders, "I just felt like a walk," she explained.

David stepped up next to her side, "It must be sort of lonely to walk all alone."

Hannah shrugged again, "I'm used to being alone."

David *thought* over his childhood and how little time he had ever spent just to himself. There were always siblings to play with, other Amish children to enjoy at events, and Lovina. Lovina had always been there for him.

Just the thought of his old friend's name sent a nagging sense of guilt through his mind.

Hadn't he promised Lovina that, when he got home, things would be different? Hadn't he promised that they would spend time together? So, what was he doing, trying to get closer to Hannah?

"David..." Hannah's soft voice brought him out of his thoughts, "Are you all right, David? I've never seen you so solemn and quiet."

David looked up at her in surprise, his face breaking out in a broad grin, "Oh, *jah*, I'm fine. I was just thinking is all."

"I didn't know you were able to do that...you know, think without saying what was going through your mind." Although Hannah's words were haughty, David *looked* up in time to catch a teasing smile cross her lips. It was the first time he had ever seen her smile and, something about it made him want to see it a thousand times more.

"Maybe it's too much time around you," David suggested, "Because I don't think you ever say anything much at all."

Hannah's tender smirk turned into a broad smile and David was, once again, captivated by her charm.

Reaching out, he gently took her elbow in his hand, "Would you do me the honor of letting me walk with ya tonight?"

Hannah was silent for a moment, studying David for all that he was worth. Finally, she nodded slowly and said, "*Jah* – I suppose that might be nice."

Chapter Five

Just as David had predicted, it was easy for Luke to find work in Kentucky. He not only spent his afternoons working on buggies in the Yoder's empty shed, but also joined the carpentry work crew lead by Lovina's father.

Lovina wasn't exactly sure how it happened, but it seemed that she and Luke were constantly thrown in the paths of one another. Lovina tried to convince herself that it was merely a coincidence, but she had to admit that it was more than that.

The longer David was gone, the less she was thinking about him and the more she was thinking about Luke.

When he wasn't busy with work, Luke frequently dropped by to help Lovina in the garden; although he wasn't a talker, there was something about his calm attitude that left Lovina yearning for more time with him.

One evening, Lovina baked a plate of her famous homemade ginger snap cookies and decided to take a few across the creek as a thank you for Luke's help in the garden.

Knocking on the shed door, she cautiously pushed it open, cheerfully announcing, "Hello! Luke! Are ya in here?"

"*Jah*, I'm here," Luke replied.

There he was, standing next to a work bench with a busted buggy wheel laid out in front of him.

"Hi there!" Lovina greeted him, suddenly feeling unsure of herself and terribly bashful, "I thought I might bring you something." Placing the plate of cookies on the work table, she watched Luke eyeball them before picking one up and putting it in his mouth.

"It's just a thank you for all the help you've been giving me," she explained.

Luke raised his eyebrows and nodded as he swallowed, "*Danki* – they're very good. You're a good baker, Lovina."

Lovina felt her heart skip a beat with his compliment. Looking at the work he was doing, she added, "Looks like you've got quite a few talents of your own."

Reaching for another cookie, Luke gave a shrug, "I keep busy for sure....but that's a good thing. I'm always thankful for the money."

Leaning back against the table, Lovina studied him in the growing darkness, "Saving back for a farm of your own?"

Luke stared straight at his work and shook his head, "No. I'm going to give my money to help out my family. I have no need of a place of my own."

"Don't you ever hope to get married and have a family?"

Luke shook his head slowly, "I'm afraid all of my dreams are gone. I plan to be alone forever."

His words broke Lovina's heart. Although he tried to sound resolved, it was easy to hear the pain in his voice.

"*Ach*, Luke," she managed to whisper with a smile, "Don't say that. You never know what might happen."

Luke took in a deep breath and then let it out slowly. Looking up to meet Lovina's eyes, he studied her for what seemed minutes before asking, "What about you? Do you think that you could ever love someone like me?"

His question took Lovina by such surprise that she almost fell over. Her eyes growing large, she looked down at the floor, her heart flooded by a million different emotions.

"I...I...Luke..." Lovina's voice was trailing in every direction but her words were making no sense at all.

"Lovina," Reaching out, Luke put his hand on top of hers, "Would you consider going with me to the singing after church this weekend?"

It felt like Lovina would not be able to breath, so many decisions were running helter-skelter through her mind. Almost a surprise to herself, she heard her voice say, "Sure. I don't see why not."

Although David had been staying busy with the horses, he still managed to make some time to help out in the store. With a beautiful girl like Hannah there, he had to find time to spend with her.

One afternoon they had received a large order of supplies and were hurrying to put them on the shelves before it would be too dark to see, even by the glow of the lantern.

"*Ach*, this is a job!" David grumbled as he hurried to put some bags of flour in their place on a shelf, "Of course this would just happen to be the night that Uncle Amos and his entire family went visiting...leaving you and me to do all the work."

Hannah smiled and shook her head, "David, you complain so much. I don't mind the work. Work keeps me busy...work keeps my mind off of...other things."

Suddenly interested, David looked up in surprise. Maybe he would finally have a chance to hear some of the secrets that were hidden away behind this mysterious girl's sad blue eyes.

"What other things?" David asked.

Hannah shrugged as she ran her fingers over a bag of sugar, "Disappointments...heartbreaks...bad decisions."

Hannah went silent, assuring David that he would hear no more of her story, but then she surprised him when she went on to clear her throat and say, "I had a boyfriend...a fiancé even."

As the words came pouring out of her mouth, it was easy to see that they were tearing her apart. Hannah closed her eyes and continued, "But things didn't work out. We were engaged but...well, I was filled with so many uncertainties. I called off the wedding before it was even announced in church. I didn't mean to end everything with him – I just needed more time to think. But I'm afraid he took it as an outright rejection. And now, I'll never have a chance with him again," Hannah reached up to wipe away the tears that were threatening to overwhelm her, "*Ach*, David, it almost breaks my heart to talk about it. I have destroyed all my chances for happiness."

Looking at her in the light of the lantern, her face clouded over with pain and tears gathering in her eyes, David felt totally broken for her. Pulling himself to his feet, he stood up straight and stepped closer to her, putting a hand on her thin shoulder.

"Hannah," he whispered her name with all the tenderness that he had been storing in his heart, "Dear Hannah...you still have a thousand chances for happiness." Reaching up, he took his thumb and brushed a tear off of her cheek.

Hannah took a deep breath and let it out slowly. Looking at him in surprise, she simply whispered, "*Danki*, David." Then she squared her shoulders and announced, "Let's get back to work."

Chapter Six

Over the next few days, David and Hannah had little time to spend together. He looked forward to ever chance he had to see her. Although their friendship had not had time to progress, David felt confident that over the rest of the summer he could easily earn himself a special place in Hannah's lonely heart.

One afternoon, David had finally found a chance to work in the dry goods store alongside Hannah when one of his cousins came rushing into the shed with a letter in his outstretched hand.

"David," the little cousin called out, "You got some mail!"

Taking the letter, David quickly recognized the handwriting as that of his younger sister, Lydia.

Ripping the seal open, David pulled out the letter, unsure why his teenage sister would even take the time to write him.

Dear David,

I don't want to bother you while you're gone, but I need to let you know something important. I've always thought that you and Lovina had something special together, although I'm not sure if you had any kind of plans for the future or an agreement. While you've been gone, Lovina has taken a spark to the very man you sent here to work – Luke Christner. Seems like they're seeing each other almost every day and last night I overheard him invite her to the singing Sunday night. She agreed to go with him.

I don't mean to stick my nose in where it doesn't belong, but I know that you were always sweet on Lovina and just thought you should know.

Your sister,

Lydia

"*Ach*," David read over the letter and then reread it again, his heart suddenly dropping into his stomach.

Lovina – with Luke? A multitude of emotions suddenly assailed David. He found himself so frustrated, almost angry at Luke for stealing his girl. How dare Luke go to David's own home and try to take the woman he loved away from him? David was hurt, so hurt, by Lovina's decision to move forward with a relationship with someone else. But, worst of all, David felt incredible guilt and sadness.

Deep in his heart, David realized that it was his own fault that Lovina and Luke were growing close. In all the time that David had been in Indiana, he had never taken the time to even write his childhood sweetheart a letter – he had just always taken for granted that she would be there for him when he returned.

While he had been busy pursing a friendship with Hannah, he had never thought that Lovina might be looking at someone else.

Reaching up, David rubbed his hand across his face, trying to gather his wits and decide what to do next.

"What is wrong, David?" Hannah asked softly as she stepped up next to him.

David balled his free hand up into a fist, fighting the urge to destroy the letter he had just received. Passing it to Hannah, he quickly explained, "I don't know how to tell you this, Hannah, but Lovina...well, she and I have always been friends. I don't mean to have led you astray in any way because I have liked you since the day we met but this..." David couldn't go on.

Hannah took the letter in her own hands and read it slowly, her eyes growing large as she went over the message again and again.

"David," she managed to breath softly, "What are you going to do?"

David brushed his hand through his hair as memories of Lovina ran across his mind, "I don't know. I just don't know." Turning, he gave the floor a hard kick with the toe of his boot.

"David," Hannah took a deep breath and shook her head slowly, "I hate to say this, but you know that we aren't meant to be together. No matter how happy we might have both been to pretend...it just isn't so. You have made my summer much more enjoyable...but it's time to get back to our real lives."

David looked down at his feet. He wanted to fight her words; he hated the idea of giving Hannah up completely. But, when he thought of his dear Lovina...he knew that he couldn't live without her.

"Go to her, David!" Hannah exclaimed, "Go to Lovina and let her know that you love her."

Taking a deep breath, David nodded his head, "I'll go call a driver right now."

Chapter Seven

David sat in the passenger seat of the truck, half-heartedly listening as his driver talked incessantly during the long trip back home. Looking out the window, David watched the scenery slowly change from the flat Amish country of Indiana to the rolling hills of Kentucky.

With each mile that passed, it seemed that David got even more nervous about his future with Lovina.

When he first started home, he had been certain that she would be glad to see him but now...well, the closer he got to her, the less sure he became. Maybe she had truly fallen for Luke and she wouldn't want to even see him. Maybe David had blown his one and only chance for true love with the only girl he ever truly cared for.

Lovina had just filled up a bucket of water and got down on her knees to scrub the kitchen floor with a scrub brush when she heard a truck pull up in the front yard.

Ach, Lovina thought to herself as she plunged her hands down into the soapy water, *Daed must have visitors.*

It was Saturday afternoon and Lovina found her mind plagued with thoughts of Luke and their upcoming date. Although she truly enjoyed spending time with him, there was something about agreeing to go on a date with him that put her mind entirely in a tizzy. As much as she liked Luke and was attracted to him, Lovina battled thoughts of David – it seemed so sad to be turning her back on their relationship with each other.

But, she reasoned to herself, when she thought back on it, she and David had never had a true relationship. Sure, he had always been a good friend to her, but it seemed that was all things were to ever be. Since he left for Indiana, she had not heard a word from him and, as sad as she was to admit it, she was starting to wonder if he would ever come home at all.

"Lovina."

The voice seemed to come out of no where. Lovina looked up in surprise, wondering if she was truly hearing a person or if it was her own imagination.

There, standing in the doorway to the kitchen, was David himself.

"David!" Lovina managed to breathe as she struggled to pull herself to her feet, "Oh, David...is that really you?"

In an instant, David had bridged the space between them. He came right to her side, nearly knocking her bucket of soapy water over in his hurry.

"Lovina," David managed to say, somewhat louder this time, "Lovina..." he seemed to want to say more, but acted as if he couldn't find the words. Reaching out, he grabbed Lovina and gathered her into his arms.

To Lovina, everything felt like a crazy dream. Pressed firmly against her old friend's body, all thoughts of Luke vanished from her mind as she let David hold her like a little girl.

"Lovina," David pulled back only long enough to kiss her on the mouth, "Lovina, I have been a total moron. I am so sorry!"

"David," Lovina managed to say as she tried to catch her breath, "David...what has happened?"

David stepped back as he struggled to gather his composure. Reaching up, he wiped away at tears that threatened to overtake him.

"Lovina," he reached out and held her hands in his own, "I have been so ignorant. I left home, anxious to find adventure and experience new things...and I almost lost the one thing that means the most to me in the world – you."

Lovina felt her heart start to melt as David poured out his soul to her, "Lovina, I love you. I love you more than I ever realized. I thought that Uncle Amos was giving me a chance to experience adventure but I think it was actually the good Lord allowing me the opportunity to realize how much I love you. Please, Lovina...I don't want to wait any longer. Say that you will marry me!"

There had never been anything that Lovina wanted more. In that instant, it felt like all of her hopes and dreams were finally coming true.

Luke.

The name entered her mind suddenly and it felt like the life was drained right out of her. Oh, but hadn't she already led him to believe that she cared for him? Hadn't she already agreed to go out on a date with him this very weekend?

"David," Lovina squeezed her dear friend's hands tightly as she looked for the right words to share her news, "David. I have been a foolish girl."

"And I have been a foolish man," David was quick to add.

Lovina smiled and shook her head, "Perhaps we've both been foolish..."

Her words were cut short as the sound of an approaching vehicle brought them both from their thoughts.

Glancing out the window, they watched together as a strange car stopped in front of the house and let out a passenger.

David felt his heart sink when he saw the visitor who was getting out of the strange car.

It was Hannah.

David thought that she had understood. What was she doing...following him all the way to Kentucky of all places? Hadn't she been the one who had said that their relationship wasn't going to work and even pushed him to return to Lovina? What was she doing here now?

David battled the urge to run forward and stop her before she could get to the house. Turning to Lovina, he struggled to find the words to explain what was surely about to come.

"Lovina..." he hurried to say, "While I was gone, I was an idiot. I hate telling you this more than you will ever know, but I got involved with a girl from Indiana. We never started to court, but we were heading in that direction when I heard that you and Luke had begun a relationship...."

As the words poured from his mouth, David watched Lovina's face turn ashen and then red with shame.

"You already know about Luke?" She managed to whisper.

David nodded his head, "That was the wake-up call I needed. That was what I needed to bring me back home. I never want to risk losing you again, Lovina!"

Lovina started to wipe tears away from her eyes, "David, I don't want to lose you either! But what you heard is true. Luke and I have grown close and are on the verge of starting a relationship. I was so foolish, David, but I was afraid I had lost you and now I don't know what to do..."

In the other room, they could hear a knock on the front door.

Wiping at her eyes, Lovina hurried to go open it with David trailing close behind. When she opened the door, Hannah was standing on the front porch, a determined look in her blue eyes.

"I need to talk to David," she announced, looking from Lovina to David.

"David," she took a deep breath, "I need to go to your house...I need to see Luke."

Luke? David was more confused than ever. Cocking his head to one side, he tried to understand where this strange twist came into play.

"You don't have to look far," the deep voice of Luke spoke out and they all turned in surprise to find that he had come up on the porch and was standing just out of view.

"Hannah," as he said the name, his voice seemed to fill with a strange sort of pain.

"*Ach*, Luke..." Hannah looked down at her black shoes as if she couldn't hold his gaze, "I have been wanting to talk to you."

Luke shook his head sadly, "I can't imagine what we would have to say to each other now."

"Luke...you know that I am a very shy girl," Hannah said in a shaky voice, "And I have let my fear get the better of me far too many times. I almost let it destroy what we had together. But Luke...I can't let that happen."

David's eyes got large as he realized that Luke must be the ex-beau that Hannah had told him about.

"I love you, Luke," Hannah announced resolutely, "I love you and I still want to be your wife...if you can ever find it in your heart to have me."

David watched Luke and held his breath, hoping that he would agree.

Stepping forward, Luke reached out and took Hannah in his arms, "I love you too, Hannah!" He exclaimed as he cupped her face in his hands, "I have always loved you and I always will." Turning to look at Lovina, he quickly tried to explain, "Lovina, I hope that you understand..."

Lovina smiled broadly as she wrapped her arms around David's waist, "It is fine, Luke. I think that things are exactly the way that they are supposed to be!"

Epilogue

Standing together at the kitchen sink, Lovina and David watched as a group of children played outside in their front yard.

"Look at those crazy things," Lovina muttered as she noticed her daughter trying to climb a tree.

"Just like us when we were little," David announced.

Lovina looked up at him and smirked, "*Jah* – and I think our little girl might have a crush on the neighbor boy, as well."

David and Lovina had now been married for ten years and had three children of their own. It had been a double wedding shared with Hannah and Luke, who decided to move to Kentucky so that Luke would continue to enjoy a steady stream of work.

David and Lovina had built their house behind his parents' place and, to their surprise, Hannah and Luke had bought a piece of farm land right across the creek.

Their children played together and it wouldn't be any surprise if someday those same children would grow up to marry one another.

David smiled broadly and gathered his wife up in his arms.

"I'm glad I went to Indiana that summer," he announced as he reached out to push a strand of her brown hair back from her face, "Because that summer showed me how much I need you in my life."

Bending over, he gave her a gentle kiss.

Life truly was as David and Lovina had always imagined it – and they were happier than they ever could have guessed possible.

THE END